Foreigner

Foreigner

Nahid Rachlin

W. W. Norton & Company

New York • *London*

Book design by Jacques Chazaud
This book is set in Avanta and Kismet
Manufacturing by Haddon Craftsmen, Inc.

Library of Congress Cataloging-in-Publication Data

Rachlin, Nahid.
  Foreigner.
  I. Title.
PZ4.R1215Fo 1978 [PS3568.A244] 813'.5'4 78–1603

ISBN 0-393-31908-3

W. W. Norton & Company, Inc.
500 Fifth Avenue, New York, N.Y. 10110
www.wwnorton.com

W. W. Norton & Company Ltd.
10 Coptic Street, London WC1A 1PU

1 2 3 4 5 6 7 8 9 0

For
Howard and Leila

Foreigner

1

As I boarded the plane at Logan Airport in Boston I paused on the top step and waved to Tony. He waved back. I pulled the window curtain beside me and closed my eyes, seeing Tony's face falling away, bitten by light. . . .

In the Teheran airport I was groggy and disoriented. I found my valise and set it on a table, where two customs officers searched it. Behind a large window people waited. The women, mostly hidden under dark *chadors,* formed a single fluid shape. I kept looking towards the window trying to spot my father, stepmother, or stepbrother, but I did not see any of them. Perhaps they were there and we could not immediately recognize each other. It had been fourteen years since I had seen them.

A young man sat on a bench beside the table, his task there not clear. He wore his shirt open and I could see bristles of dark hair on his chest. He was making shadow pictures on the floor—a rabbit, a bird—and then dissolving the shapes between his feet. Energy emanated from his hands, a crude, confused energy. Suddenly he looked at me, staring into my eyes. I turned away.

I entered the waiting room and looked around. Most people had left. There was still no one for me. What could possibly have happened? Normally someone would be there —a definite effort would be made. I fought to shake off my groggy state.

A row of phones stood in the corner next to a handicraft shop. I tried to call my father. There were no phone books and the information line rang busy, on and on.

I went outside and approached a collection of taxis. The drivers stood around, talking. "Can I take one of these?" I asked.

The men turned to me but no one spoke.

"I need a taxi," I said.

"Where do you want to go?" one of the men asked. He was old with stooped shoulders and a thin, unfriendly face. I gave him my father's address.

"That's all the way on the other side of the city." He did not move from his spot.

"Please . . . I have to get there somehow."

The driver looked at the other men as if this were a group project.

"Take her," one of them said. "I would take her myself but I have to get home." He smiled at me.

"All right, get in," the older man said, pointing to a taxi.

In the taxi, he turned off the meter almost immediately. "You have to pay me 100 *tomans* for this."

"That much?"

"It would cost you more if I left the meter on."

There was no point arguing with him. I sat stiffly and looked out. We seemed to be floating in the sallow light cast by the street lamps. Thin old sycamores lined the sidewalks. Water flowed in the gutters. The smoky mountains surrounding the city, now barely visible, were like a dark ring. The streets were more crowded and there were many more tall western buildings than I had remembered. Cars sped by, bouncing over holes, passing each other recklessly, honking. My taxi driver also drove badly and I had visions of an accident, of being maimed.

We passed through quieter, older sections. The driver slowed down on a narrow street with a mosque at its center, then stopped in front of a large, squalid house. This was the street I had lived on for so many years; here I had played hide-and-seek in alleys and hallways. I had a fleeting sensation that I had never left this street, that my other life with Tony had never existed.

I paid the driver, picked up my valise, and got out. On the cracked blue tile above the door, "Akbar Mehri," my father's name, was written.

I banged the iron knocker several times and waited. In the light of the street lamps I could see a beggar with his jaw twisted sitting against the wall of the mosque. Even though it was rather late, a hum of prayers, like a moan, rose from the mosque. A Moslem priest came out, looked past the beggar and spat on the ground. The doors of the house across the street were open. I had played with two little girls, sisters, who lived there. I could almost hear their voices, laughter. The April air was mild and velvety against my skin but I shivered at the proximity to my childhood.

A pebble suddenly hit me on the back. I turned but could not see anyone. A moment later another pebble hit my leg and another behind my knee. More hit the ground. I turned again and saw a small boy running and hiding in the arched hallway of a house nearby.

I knocked again.

There was a thud from the inside, shuffling, and then soft footsteps. The door opened and a man—my father—

stood before me. His cheeks were hollower than I had re-called, the circles under his eyes deeper, and his hair more evenly gray. We stared at each other.

"It's you!" He was grimacing, as though in pain.

"Didn't you get my telegram?"

He nodded. "We waited for you for two hours this morning in the airport. What happened to you?"

I was not sure if he was angry or in a daze. "You must have gotten the time mixed up. I meant nine in the *evening.*"

My father stretched his hands forward, about to embrace me but, as though struck by a shyness, he let them drop at his sides. "Come in now."

I followed him inside. I too was in the grip of shyness, or something like it.

"I thought you'd never come back," he said.

"I know, I know."

"You aren't even happy to see me."

"That's not true. I'm just . . ."

"You're shocked. Of course you are."

He went towards the rooms, arranged in a semicircle, on the other side of the courtyard. A veranda with columns extended along several of the rooms. Crocuses, unpruned rosebushes, and pomegranate trees filled the flower beds. A round pool of water stood between the flower beds. The place seemed cramped, untended. But still it was the same house. Roses would blossom, sparrows would chirp at the edge of the pool. At dawn and dusk the voice of the muezzin would mix with the noise of people coming from and going to the nearby bazaars.

We went up the steps onto the veranda and my father opened the door to one of the rooms. He stepped inside and guilt or the sacrifices the leaders of Islam had made. They would cry as if at their own irrevocable guilt and sorrow.

We were together in the kitchen. Darius, Ziba, my father—they seemed at once familiar and remote like figures in dreams.

Ziba, her eyes still shrewd and slipping frequently into disapproval, lips thin and prim, hair frizzy from a permanent, breasts flat under the loose, white robe. A woman in her late forties but looking older, with deep frown lines on her forehead and creases all over her face as if a layer of anxiety had imprinted itself on her. Darius, wearing his stained work clothes—his dark, persistent gaze, protruding forehead, heavy sensual lips. The last I had heard, he worked as a garage mechanic instead of in my father's fabric shop in Sabzi Bazaar as they had once both hoped. And my father, crouching on a chair, eyes almost hidden under his thick eyebrows as if he were trying to avoid confrontation with me.

"I'd have had something better for you to eat if I knew you'd be here tonight," Ziba said, mixing with a spoon the leftover *abgoosht* she was warming on the stove.

"Don't worry about me. I'm not hungry." Although I had eaten little on the plane I had no appetite.

"She isn't a stranger," Darius said.

But I *was* a stranger, with people I had not seen for so long and hardly knew any more. I looked around the imitation modern kitchen—redone since I had left—with plastic chairs made to look like wood, a brown formica table, a flimsy gas stove and, instead of the wooden icebox, an old refrigerator with its enamel chipped. The gold-colored curtains were soiled with spots of grease.

14

turned on the light. I paused for a moment, afraid to
the threshold. I could smell it: must, jasmin, rosew
garlic, vinegar, recalling my childhood. Shut doors with
fused noises behind them, slippery footsteps, black, go
eyed cats staring from every corner, indolent afterr
when people reclined on mattresses, forbidden subjec
casionally reaching me—talk about a heavy flow of
strual blood, sex inflicted by force, the last dark word
woman on her death bed.

My father disappeared into another room. I heard
whispering and then someone said loudly, "She's h
Footsteps approached. In the semidarkness of a doorv
the far end of the room two faces appeared and then ar
face, like three moons, staring at me.

"Feri, what happened?" a woman's voice asked,
figure stepped forward. I recognized my stepmother,
She wore a long, plain cotton nightgown.

"The time got mixed up, I guess." My voice so
feeble and hesitant.

A man laughed and walked into the light too. It v
stepbrother, Darius. He grinned at me, a smile discon
from his eyes.

"Let's go to the kitchen," my father said. "So th
can eat something."

They went back through the same doorway and
lowed them. We walked through the dim, inter
rooms in tandem. In one room all the walls were
with black cloth, and a throne, also covered with
cloth, was set in a corner—for monthly prayers when
borhood women would come in and a Moslem pri
invited to give sermons. The women would wail ar
their chests in these sessions as the priest talked abou

"What did you do that for, not come back for so long?" my father said, his eyes still cast downward.

"I was busy, time went by—it didn't seem like so long." I couldn't seem to find the words. "And my work—it's hard to get away from it." I was a biologist, a researcher in a consulting firm near Boston. Although I worked hard, building a career, my refusal to return for visits, in spite of my father's pressure, had taken an effort on my part. I had tried to forget my past. But gradually, after years, that had no longer been possible. Little by little I had been filled with a sense of futility and restlessness. Vague dissatisfactions with work, with Tony, with people I knew had set on me.

"You're back now," my father said, as though trying to avoid unpleasantness.

"It seems she never left," Darius said, punching me gently on my side.

"But you look different," my father said. "You look Western."

My hair was short, just to the nape of my neck in a blunt cut. I had plucked my eyebrows so that they were almost straight, making my eyes seem larger than they were and my face more angular. I wore a silk blouse, a scooped-neck sweater, and slacks.

"You don't expect me not to have changed," I said.

"She's just as thin as she used to be," Ziba said, putting a bowl of *abgoosht* and a slab of gravel-baked bread before me.

I began to eat reluctantly.

"She was thin as a child," my father said. "Thin as a reed."

"We'll have to feed her well," Darius said.

"Why didn't you bring your husband with you?" my father asked.

"He had work to do."

"He teaches college, right?"

I nodded. Tony taught urban planning at a university in Cambridge.

"A college professor," Darius said with a touch of mockery. "Do you have any pictures of him? You never sent one to us."

My father had objected so strongly to the news that I wanted to marry Tony—an American—that I had kept most of the business to myself.

I took out a photograph of Tony from my wallet and handed it to Darius. In the picture Tony sat on a swivel chair in his study in our house. Behind him there was a shelf filled with books, in front of him a formica desk with a typewriter on it. He sat smiling into the camera. He seemed to be smiling at me. A wave like a distant breeze touched me. The brittleness that had begun to mark his behavior and the defiance that often lurked in his eyes did not show in the photograph. When we had first met he was full of optimism.

"He's a bit faded looking. It must be that blond hair," Darius said.

Ziba took the picture, holding it upside down. She did not have her glasses on and she squinted to see. "Oh, he certainly is white-washed."

"How did you get married? Did they have *aghounds* there?" Darius asked.

"It wasn't a religious wedding."

"Not religious? What does that mean?"

"It was a civil ceremony."

"You aren't really married to him then, you've been living in sin," Ziba said, her voice becoming shrill.

"We must find her a husband while she's here," Darius said.

"And a wife for you. You'll have a double marriage," Ziba said.

"I already have a husband," I said.

Ziba sighed. "There is so much wrong in the world."

My father shook his head, looking melancholy.

We fell into silence. The house was silent. I felt a heavy weight tugging at my heart. I reminded myself that I would be there only for two weeks.

I felt an even heavier weight when I was alone in my room, the same one I had had years before. It was an austere room with dust gathered on the few items of furniture—a sagging bed, a faded paisley rug, a chest and a chair.

I went to the tiny window overlooking a main street and opened it. Outside, a cloth hung from two trees, advertising a rug store. Wide gutters, with water rippling in them ran along both sides of the street. A woman wearing a *chador* stood under a lamppost, moving her head from side to side, on the watch.

Somewhere a man sang,
"Come and join me. We'll go to the town of Ray,
To tear down mountains, to build fountains,
Come with me, we'll sail up a river."

I noticed a clay unicorn on the mantel. I picked it up and examined it. The black eyes had faded and its horn was missing. I had had a similar one as a child and wondered if this was it.

After a while I went to bed. Shadows surrounded me as I lay there with the light turned off and the curtains drawn.

When I was a child I had wakened at night to odd noises, horrifying shapes in the dark, faraway laughter, a cobweb structure clinging to everything. I would go cold. Sometimes I would get up and crawl into my father's bed.

"What's the matter? What are you doing here?" my father had asked the first time.

"I was afraid."

"Of what? Did anyone hurt you?"

"No, no, just the dark."

"You aren't a child any more. You musn't be afraid." He had kissed me on the cheek and turned away. I hugged his side and remained that way as though movement would destroy the mood that enveloped us. I could feel his fingers tapping on my hand, then becoming still as his breathing grew regular and heavy.

He had been a gentle, lenient father. Then disagreements and harshnesses had started between us.

Now I was back in that room and felt the fear once again.I pulled the patchwork quilt over my head and tried to sleep.

2

The restaurant where we went for lunch the next day was a small, dim place with frescoes of Rostam and Sohrab, legendary heroes, on the wall. The air was filled with the aroma of *kebab,* marinated in onion and tumeric. A faucet dripped somewhere and dishes clattered. There were only a few other customers.

Darius popped his knuckles. He seemed agitated and there was a blue mark under his eyes. Suddenly he leaned towards me. "Touch my head. There's a lump here. Go ahead, touch it." He took my hand and brought it to his head.

I could feel the lump under my fingers. "What happened?"

"I had a fight with my partner. He's always looking for trouble. He eggs me on."

"You need to get married," Ziba said. "You have too much energy to go without a wife."

The waiter, a thin young man with a well-trimmed mustache and black eyes, came over, rubbing his greasy hands on his apron. Darius gave him the order, adding boisterously, "I want you to bring the best of what you have. My sister has just returned from America."

"O.K., O.K.," the waiter said in English. He laughed and walked away.

My eyes had adjusted to the gloom and I could see that what had seemed like a bundle of laundry in a corner was an old man propped up against the wall, a sheet covering him up to the neck. A young boy sat in front of him, spooning food into his mouth and cleaning up, with a handkerchief, what dripped down his chin. Then the boy kneeled down, lifted the old man on his back and carried him through a curtain to a back room.

The waiter brought the food and we began to eat.

My father was quiet and looked moody with his eyelids drooping and the flesh under his chin sagging.

"Are you all right?" I asked.

He shook his head and said nothing.

"Don't you feel well?" I persisted.

He put one hand under his chin and the other on the buckle of his belt. Then as though something had been resolved in him, he leaned over and smiled at me. "Poor child," he said.

I looked at him, puzzled.

"To have lived in a foreign country for so long."

"But I chose that."

"Chose!" my father said.

"I don't know what's so sad about it. Most young people like to go to America," Ziba said, avoiding my eyes. "Not many people get that chance."

I was relieved when the conversation was interrupted as the waiter came over to clear the table. "O.K., O.K.," he repeated.

"Why don't you sing a song for us?" Darius said to the waiter. "You have such a nice voice."

"I can't do that now."

"Please, for my sake. I'm one of your old customers."

"Come on, come on," said three men who were sitting at a table close to ours.

The waiter looked around for a moment as if trying to decide. Then he stood between the two tables and, tilting his head upward, half closing his eyes, began to sing an old-fashioned song.

"Your skin is white like the moon, your hair black like
   the sky,
Your hands are round and plump, resembling ripe
   fruit . . ."

His face had caught the mood of the song. It looked sad, love-stung, and his voice was nasal, drawing out the song as if it were a dirge.

He stopped and everyone applauded.

"You'll get your reward," Darius said to him with emphasis.

The waiter nodded and walked away, into the kitchen.

One of the men at the next table kept staring at me, a sleazy smile hovering on his face, his gold tooth glistening. His black eyes were shadowed by dark lashes and his dark hair was combed in a pompadour. I looked away from him, then glanced back. He was still staring.

Darius noticed the man's expression. "Did you see that? He has the nerve to flirt with you while I'm sitting right here."

"It's all right. No harm to it."

"You don't care? Well I do." His face had taken on

a frightening rigidity. "If he keeps that up I'll crush his bones. I'll pluck his eyes out."

The man arched his eyebrows.

Darius jumped up and went towards him. "You'd better get up and answer for yourself."

The man got up, grinning uncomfortably. They stood face to face, looking into each other's eyes, as if each were gauging the other's strength. I watched nervously. "What do you think you're doing flirting with my sister?" Darius grasped the man's arms.

"Please leave him alone. I really don't care," I said.

"It's his pride he has to defend," Ziba said.

"Easy, easy," my father said, lifting up his heavy bulk with difficulty.

"Stop it!" I cried.

Darius tightened his grip and the two men struggled together. My father and the man's companions tried without success to pull them apart. The waiter came back from the kitchen. "What's going on, what's happening?" he asked.

No one answered him.

He took hold of the man's waist and managed to pull him away from Darius. "Tell me. I'll be the judge."

"I'm going to kill him," Darius threatened, grabbing the man again.

One of the companions whispered something to the waiter. The waiter turned to Darius. "He's young and stupid. Let him go and he'll leave the restaurant."

Darius hesitated, then let go. The three men went back to their table, picked up their jackets, and left without glancing at us.

"If it wasn't for the women's presence, I'd have spilled his guts," Darius said, taking his seat. He was sweating and breathed heavily.

The waiter said, "Your sister is used to such things. In America men and women hold hands freely on the streets."

"Do you want me to give you a beating too?" Darius said, a vein on his neck standing out.

"No offense intended," the waiter said, walking away swiftly.

All the way home I was silent, troubled by the incident. Darius had always had a way of putting me off balance. There was that day when I was climbing the stairs leading up to the roof and Darius grasped my arm from behind, bringing me to a halt immediately. Even though he was a year younger than me I always viewed him as older and stronger.

"What were you doing in father's bed last night?"

"I was afraid so I went there."

"You just went there?" The expression on his face reflected something like anger or greed.

"I was afraid of the dark."

He leaned forward and put his hands on the wall behind me. I tried to get out of the circle of his arms but he held me back, pressing his body against mine.

"Where do you think you're going?" he said, a flirtatious glint coming into his eyes.

"Let me go, let me go. I'm going to scream." That was a feeble threat—I knew my father was out and Ziba wouldn't pay attention.

"You wouldn't dare," he said, still smiling.

Then, suddenly, he pulled me to himself.

"Let me go."

"Don't worry," he said, his voice becoming gentle. "I'm not going to do anything to you."

His grasp became tighter. I struggled.

"Wait just one moment," he whispered, his mouth near my ear. Then he began to move his body up and down against me as he put one hand under my clothes on my buttocks and the other on my back. He was breathing heavily.

His grasp was so strong that I could not move—my body became frozen.

He stopped abruptly, letting go, and ran down the stairs without looking at me.

I stayed there, leaning against the wall for a few moments, trying to bring blood and motion back into myself.

When I came down into the courtyard, I was struck by how light it still was, with the sun shining high above the trees and reflecting in the doorway, and how menacing the silence was. I went into my room, shut the door and stood in front of the mirror, seeing my face as in a nightmare— yellow and dry and stiff. I took off my dress and examined my body as though aware of it for the first time.

I put my clothes back on and went out of the house, full of an excess of energy which made me want to cry or run, get lost in crowds. I turned to the right, towards a little bazaar. Darius was standing near the entrance with a group of his friends—gruff, frightening boys, the kind who would sometimes block the way of girls on the street.

"Where are you going?" Darius asked as calmly as though nothing had happened.

I walked rapidly past him, into the crowded bazaar.

Soon after that incident I supposed myself in love with

a boy who lived nearby. In the afternoon, when everyone went down for a nap, he sat in the hot sun on the roof of his house, letting his pigeons fly and watching them circle in the air and come back. He was lean, dark, and had startling gray eyes. I would sit by the window of my room and watch him. When he noticed me he sat closer to the edge of the roof, glancing towards me frequently. Sometimes we stared into each other's eyes. When I passed his house I would walk slowly, hoping to catch sight of him.

Once he was standing in the hallway as I approached. He beckoned to me to come in. The wave of his hand was like a magnet and I followed it, and in that dim, small hallway felt it on my cheek. I must draw away, run out, I thought, but I stood there and he held my hand and we kissed for a long time. Shyly I put my arms around his waist, feeling my thighs against his. An erotic sensation came over me. Although I could not understand its nature, it made me tremble in his arms.

We became more and more daring. We began to meet in distant neighborhoods where we would not be recognized, for an afternoon movie or ice cream in a modern restaurant. We would mostly see American or European movies. Gregory Peck, Jennifer Jones, or Silvana Mangano moved before me with messages from other worlds. Always we would hold hands. Once or twice he kissed me.

I was filled with anxiety that perhaps I had lost my virginity, that no one would be willing to marry me. My knowledge on the subject was vague and my friends were equally ignorant. I set out to see a gynecologist in a clinic I had noticed once on one of my excursions to the other side of the town. I told the receptionist that I wanted to be examined but did not want anyone to know about it. She shook her head and asked no further questions. I sat on a bench along with several other young girls who were there with their mothers or aunts or cousins. One of the girls was crying. I was very stiff and ashamed, and tried not to look at anyone.

In a few moments a nurse—a middle-aged woman—came in and led me to a room. She asked me to undress, put on a robe and lie on a cot. I went through the process of getting undressed and lay on the cot, staring at the ceiling and counting to make time pass faster.

The doctor, a woman, came in, holding some shiny instruments. She was young and pleasant-looking with a smile lingering on her face.

"What's the problem?" she asked.

"I wonder if . . . if . . ."

"I know. You want to know if you're a virgin."

I nodded, blushing deeply.

"That's a common fear these days among young girls. Have you had intercourse with a boy?"

The question puzzled me. I was silent.

"No?" she asked.

"I kissed and held hands with a boy . . . two boys." I was counting Darius. Tears filled my eyes.

She laughed. "That's not enough to do anything to your virginity, but you can break the hymen on rare occasions, by exercise. I'll examine you anyway."

The tears spilled out of my eyes as I tensed at her touch, her gaze at parts of me that I thought must be permanently kept from scrutiny.

"Relax, relax. Here, I'm finished. You have nothing to worry about. Everything is fine. You can get married now without being afraid."

I sighed with relief. I was bouncy all the way back. But then I had no desire to see the boy again. The last encounter I had with him was on a day when I was coming home from school with a group of girls.

We were all wearing the gray school uniforms. The day was hot and a mass of locusts buzzed, travelling through the dirty haze that hung in the air. We were approaching his house. I broke away from my friends and began to walk fast. I suspected that the boy might be waiting for me and did not want anyone to notice. As I reached the door to his house I saw him standing in the dim hallway. He beckoned to me. I looked at him, shook my head, and went on. Either he was crushed by my behavior or he himself had lost interest, because he did not persist in trying to see me.

I dreamed of escape into a different world. I asked my father, repeatedly, to let me go abroad. I begged or threatened alternately until he softened. Later he even became eager for me to leave, as if he had thought of the idea himself. Perhaps he hoped that an education would protect me from some passion or impulse that he might have sensed in me.

When I had finished high school and was about to leave for a college in the States, Darius came into my room. A cigarette smouldered between his lips. As I packed he watched the smoke as though afraid of other confrontations. The usual roughness had disappeared from his face.

"You'll write, won't you?" he asked.

I did not reply, thinking I would never write to him. And I did not.

Now I was walking beside Darius, uneasy with him as always, pretending to listen to my father and Ziba as they chatted. At home I excused myself to shower and take a nap even though it was unusual for me to sleep during the day. Ziba had heated the bathroom water in the morning.

The shower was a small cemented area off the kitchen. The water alternated from too hot to too cold but I stood under it for a long time. My upper back and chest hurt—an elusive pain, hard to pin down. It was like a muscular pain but I kept worrying that an illness might keep me bedridden for days. I was no longer immune to the germs here.

I found a bar of soap and a yellowish shampoo on a shelf. The soap was of a poor quality and would not lather. My father could have done more to make the place comfortable, I thought. He was not poor certainly, although he had made sacrifices to send me to school in the States. The house, once beautiful, was in decay now, like the neighborhood. But this was the house and the neighborhood my father was used to. Always reluctant to make changes, he would never think of moving.

A shadow appeared behind the translucent window on the shower door, covering it for an instant and disappearing. It was a featureless silhouette but I thought I recognized Darius's face. I jumped against the wall and crossed my hands on my chest protectively. I was shaking with anger and shock. Then the incident seemed like a hallucination, the way the shape spread over the window, becoming larger and denser and then dissolving altogether.

3

Ziba sat behind a manual sewing machine in the living room, making seams on the dress I had brought for her. It was too large, she said, and she was determined to alter it before the relatives came. Around her lay a pile of other presents I had brought. She had examined them and tried some on to decide which relative should get what. The activity had made her cheerful—for the first time since I had come.

The room was covered with elaborately designed rugs and cushions. It had no windows. Rose-colored curtains hung on the doors opening into the courtyard. I leaned against the cushion near a half-opened door and looked at the goldfish in the pool outside. A mourning dove perched on the parapet, cooing. The smell of spicy food wafted in from the kitchen. My back and chest still hurt. I watched for signs of fever but the pain remained in the muscles. It could be from the long trip, I thought.

I regretted not having brought work to do—I had already read the biology journals I had brought with me. Time stretched ahead of me, dead-centered and nightmarish. I kept looking at my watch, amazed that only ten minutes or half an hour had passed, thinking how Tony and I would go into a state of frenzy if one of us or someone else was ten minutes late. At the beginning, when we planned to meet, I was usually at fault. Once Tony was so angry that he would not speak to me while I followed him for the fifteen-block walk to his university. I had fallen far behind and stood laughing in exasperation.

Now I picked up a magazine and tried to read it. I realized my reading of Persian had grown rusty. It was a gossip magazine—belonging to Darius probably—with articles about Elizabeth Taylor or Omar Sharif. The advertisements showed Western-looking models.

Ziba bit off the thread and stood up to try on the dress. "I wonder if I should wear such a bright color. I'm an old woman. I haven't worn colors for so long." She held the bottom of her dress and turned around like a little girl, looking at herself in the mirror behind a door.

"It's good with your dark eyes and hair," I said. She looked younger in the reddish dress.

She picked up a perfume bottle from the mantel and dabbed her chest with it. Patches of brown stained her dress and the air became full of the strong scent of jasmin.

"Try some on." She tilted the bottle on her finger again and put some perfume on my sleeve before I could resist. My father walked in, wearing the striped blue and white shirt I had given to him. (I had given a similar one to Darius.) He said, "Your uncle and aunt are here."

My father's younger brother and his wife appeared in the courtyard. They took off their shoes before entering the room. Ziba reached for her *chador* and we both got up to greet them. My uncle embraced me awkwardly, then my aunt did.

"You're back after all these years," he said. His voice still sounded young and strong, vibrating with emotion. Except for the graying hair and a few lines on his face, he was very much the same as years before—swarthy looking with alert dark eyes and oiled hair, neatly combed and parted in the middle. He wore khaki pants and a checkered shirt with the top buttons open.

He had been a rebellious young man, staying up late, coming home drunk and throwing up. I remembered riding with him on a train—he wore a striped blue suit and a red tie, his cheeks were flushed. I sat on one side of him and on the other side sat a young woman, wearing a thin, transparent *chador*. It was night and only a small lamp lit our carriage. When we reached our station she got up and walked away. My uncle and I got up also and went in the other direction. He stopped by a shop and bought me a rag doll and some candies. He handed them to me, winked, and pinched my cheek. "You won't say anything to anyone about her, will you? She was a nice lady, wasn't she?"

At another time he stood in front of a mirror, shaving while I watched. He put down the razor, turned to me, and said, "I'll work all my life and be nowhere, no one, just a civil servant." A moment later (or was it another day?), he added, "I wish I could live somewhere else, somewhere more lively."

"What made you disappear like that?" his wife, Munir, asked me now. She was a gentle, pretty woman with soft brown hair piled in curls around her face.

"I didn't mean to disappear." I smiled.

"You went away and forgot about us," my uncle said, sitting next to me.

"I really didn't forget."

"I sent her to America to learn something and come

31

back. Instead she went there and forgot about us," my father said as if he had not heard my feeble attempt to defend myself. A familiar film of pain spread over his eyes.

"You didn't do that even for your son," my aunt said.

"No, Darius was a wild boy."

"He said studying would make all his hair fall out," I said.

"You were very smart from the time you were a baby," my father said. "Did you know that you talked in full sentences before you could walk? Once you learned how to walk you went on and on. You learned to walk but not how to stop."

Everyone laughed. I realized from the harshness of my laughter how tense I was. My father had rested all his hopes and expectations on me rather than Darius. He had hoped I would get an education, that I would come back. He had hoped perhaps that I would marry an Iranian man and have children.

"Where is Darius?" my aunt asked.

"At the garage probably, looking out at girls."

Everyone laughed again.

Ziba picked up a scarf and a tie and gave them to my aunt and uncle.

"I haven't worn a tie for so long," my uncle said, studying the gift closely. "But I'll keep this as a souvenir from Feri."

His wife thanked me and folded the scarf, putting it neatly in a corner.

My uncle began to talk in an animated way, telling me stories about my childhood, squeezing my thigh, pinching my arm. He tried to use some of the English words he had learned in the oil refinery company where he worked.

"You used to love your uncle so," his wife said, looking at her husband with adoration. "You followed him around. You wanted to be with him all the time."

"That's right," I said, thinking of the energy that had always drawn me to him.

"I was so happy for you when your father decided to send you to college abroad," my uncle said. He suddenly seemed agitated, beads of sweat gathered on his forehead, his words came out rapidly, jumbled. "Everyone works and works over there, in America, all for the dollar. More work and more dollar. They have so much money and yet they keep running after more. Here no one is willing to work for more than a few hours a day. Human feelings come first here. I work only enough to make a living. Now, as my children grow older, I work a little harder." His body grew rigid. "Tell me, why didn't your husband come with you? Does he consider our country beneath him?" His hand was wet with sweat as he touched my arm.

"He was busy and I wanted to come alone."

"You've become one of them—you abandoned your family." He winked at me and laughed. "I'm only joking."

Two women, wearing black *chadors*, appeared in the courtyard and came into the living room.

I recognized the thin, sallow-faced woman as my cousin Simin. She and I had been good friends as children.

She held me to herself and we kissed on both cheeks.

"Feri, what happened to you? You just disappeared," the older woman—my father's sister and Simin's mother— asked, her head shaking a little. She had only four large rotting teeth in the front of her mouth and this had made her cheeks sink in and her chin protrude. She came over and we kissed.

33

We all sat around the room.

Ziba gave my aunt a dark, somber dress and Simin a nightgown. "These are for you."

Simin held the nightgown before her and smiled. "What a pretty color."

"I can't wear this," my aunt said, pushing the dress away. "You shouldn't wear that nightgown either, for that matter. They have been made and handled by the infidel."

"We can wash them and then wear them," Simin suggested.

"My sister has always been too extreme," my uncle said. He had been quiet for the last few moments and his cheeks were flushed.

"I'm on my way to my grave. I have to be careful—I can't make blunders any more."

Darius came into the room. There was a commotion as everyone greeted him. He sat down next to my uncle.

"Maybe you can get your husband to come over too and live here," Simin said to me.

"He can't," I said. "There's nothing here for him to do."

"What, him? She isn't married to him," my father said with sudden energy. The exertion made him cough for a long time.

"She isn't married to him?" Simin asked, puzzled.

"They have no *aghounds* there," Ziba said.

My aunt and Simin focused their eyes on me with curiosity.

"They have other things there, I'm sure," Simin said, smiling at me.

"They had no religious wedding at all," my father said. "Right? A clerk wrote something and you signed it."

34

"We have to do something about that," Darius said menacingly.

"Do we have to talk about these things?" I felt a bitterness in the back of my mouth, a strong urge to get up and leave.

My aunt closed her eyes and shook her head several times as if she could not bear the intensity of the information.

Ziba got up and said, "I'm going to get some lunch for us," and my aunts arose to help her. They left the room and came back with dishes, silverware, and a cloth. They spread the cloth on the floor and arranged the dishes on it. They went back and forth, bringing in saffron rice, soup, stews, pickles. . . . They insisted that I should not help since I was a guest.

We all sat around the cloth to eat, except for my uncle who went towards the adjacent room—the link to the courtyard. His body swung as he walked, his hands dangled at his sides. I felt alarm as I watched him without quite knowing why. After a moment I got up and went into the other room and saw my uncle disappearing into the courtyard. The room was very quiet and I could hear the ticking of a clock. My pocketbook which I had hung on a hook swayed slightly. Its top was open. I reached for it and fumbled through it. My wallet was gone.

My father came in. I must have looked strange. He asked immediately, "Is something wrong?"

"My wallet."

"I thought he might have done it again." He went pale. "You musn't let anyone know about it. I've always tried to save his face. He takes everything he can get hold of."

My uncle came to the doorway. My eyes locked with his

35

for an instant in a state of shock—both of us were stunned.

He dropped his eyes and said, "I went to wash my hands."

"Did you take her wallet?" my father asked in a voice more resigned than accusing.

My uncle's lips trembled with small twitches, but he did not say anything. He went towards the hook, his body moving mechanically. He bent down and I could see the wallet slipping out of his hand onto the floor. "Here it is, the wallet is right here." He stood up. "I just went to wash my hands."

Without exchanging another word we went back to the living room. Everyone was eating and no one asked any questions. My uncle sat on the same side of the cloth as I, sheltered behind a row of elbows and shoulders, his face hidden from me. The room was full of traps.

4

Afterwards, in my room, I could still see my uncle's face as he had dropped the wallet. I should pity him, I said to myself. He is a frustrated man, a person whose energy and liveliness have gone sour. His stealing is a cry for attention. The rationalization did not help.

I tried, futilely, to recall the sense of urgency I had had about the trip. The plan had begun to form in my mind one late afternoon as I stood behind the picture window of our living room in Lexington, looking out at the grass-covered backyard, acutely aware of a stillness all around me. The trees, a bird sitting on a branch, the backyards of neighbors, seemed to have gone to sleep or frozen to death. Color had bled out of them. How different this was from that other world, I had thought. Our sun-choked, dust-swept court-yard, the melancholy sunsets and hazy noons. The hum of prayers pouring out of mosques, a child climbing an ancient tree. Uncertainty, a mystery in the air.

That night I had dreamt of Iran, something that I had not done since I married Tony. In the dream I was sitting in the hollowed-out stump of a tree in our courtyard. It was a very clear day and all the flowers and leaves were vividly outlined in the sun. Then the air suddenly changed; a hard wind began to blow and it quickly turned into a hurricane. Someone was walking towards me in the darkened air, calling my name, asking for help. I jumped out of my enclosure and ran towards the figure whose voice became more and more desperate—a tiny, featureless figure with its hands stretched out, trying to move forward but not able to. As I came closer I could see that the figure was someone very much like me, only she was smaller and younger.

"Who are you?" I asked.

"Don't you know me?"

I shook my head.

She began to laugh, trembling all over, her features becoming distorted and frightening. It was as if I were looking at my image in a broken mirror.

I woke, my heart thumping rapidly.

Now in Iran, things had quickly reversed—what had seemed mysterious was menacing and what had seemed sterile in the States appeared to be orderly, almost peaceful.

I missed, as if it were taken away from me permanently, my white shingled house in Lexington supplied with modern comforts, my neighbors, their talk about books, the latest movies, or plays. The green backyard, the smell of cut grass. The voices of Maria Muldaur or Steven Stills pouring out of the phonograph. My laboratory overlooking the Charles River. I spent long hours there every day, charting changes in the viscosity of hormones and enzymes, studying the abnormal growth of cells in rats. Tony, sitting across from me at night, working or examining a book he had just bought —he collected first editions of scientific books.

Impulsively I decided to get my exit visa and leave before the two weeks had passed. It would take time for the visa to be issued, a few days anyway.

The next morning, as I was heading towards the outside door, my father called after me, "Where are you going?"

I turned around. He was wearing a badly cut, somber looking suit. A watch on a chain hung from his trousers.

"To the passport bureau. I want to get my exit visa."

"Already? You aren't serious, are you. You're angry at me or maybe at your uncle?"

"I'm not angry. I just have to get back sooner than I had planned. I have work to do—and there are things I forgot."

"I can see you're angry—I don't blame you. But he loves you. He must have gone home and cried for what he did. He can't help himself when he steals like that. It's a sickness."

"I'll come back sooner next time. Or you could come and visit me. You'd like that." I knew or rather hoped that he would not accept the invitation. I would have to attend to him as a child if he came. He did not know English or how to drive. Then, feeling selfish, I said, "You must come."

He shook his head almost sadly. "I'm an old man. It isn't easy for me to travel. Besides I have work too." Then he grew angry. "Why did you come then, if you were going to run back immediately? You remind me of her, your mother. *She* had no regard for me either or else she wouldn't have left like that for another man."

The reference to my mother seemed suspended between us; I could feel my ears ringing. It had been years since anyone had mentioned her. She had remained sealed inside me like an illusion too real to discard altogether. My mother had simply disappeared one day, when I was eight years old. My father and my relatives always said the same thing in answer to my incessant questions about her—that she had responded to a religious calling and had gone away to devote herself to God. No one knew where she was. Then after a while, no one wanted to talk about her and she had gradually become a dark memory.

"What are you talking about? What do you mean she went away with another man?"

My father sat down on the bricks around the flower bed. Crocuses, roses. A whiff of my childhood. My mother standing in a doorway and calling me, "Feri, come in and eat," or waving her hand, "Watch out, you're going to fall." She was a large woman and had a mass of dark, wavy hair that she usually wore loose down her back.

"No one ever told me anything about this," I said to my father.

"Why inflict a child with shame?"

"Who was this other man?"

"Do you really want to know? A scoundrel who soon abandoned her."

"Where is she now? Does she live in Teheran?" I was raising my voice.

"Do you think I've kept track?" he said listlessly, getting up and brushing off the dirt from his pants.

Ziba came into the courtyard. "What's going on?" Her hair was henna red, and she had remnants of mascara smeared around her eyes. "The neighbors can hear you." She turned to me. "Do you have to stir things up?"

Her voice had the unsparing coldness I recalled from the past.

How I had recoiled from her that very first day she had come to live with us. She sat by a samovar, holding a cube of sugar between her teeth and sucking tea through it. She had regarded me with a shrewd, judging look and, taking out the sugar cube, she said, "Come here, let me kiss you." I was wearing a full dress and as I began to walk it seemed to wrap around my legs. "She hates me, I can tell," she had said.

She would often be sitting in the courtyard when I got back from school, letting henna dry on her hair and fingernails. She would have a series of errands for me to do.

"Water stopped running in the faucet today. I want you to pump some from the cistern."

"Not now. I'm too tired."

"Tired! You haven't done anything all day. You've just been playing at school."

"I worked at school."

"You don't know what work is. I used to do all the housework and take care of five brothers and sisters when I was your age." Her voice was low, barely hiding hostility.

I went to the hand pump in the corner of the courtyard and filled the pail with water.

When I left for the United States she had stood in the same spot. "It will be peaceful here with you gone. We'll have some rest," she had said. I ignored her, consoled by my own fantasies. Now I was face to face with her again but was no longer protected by those fantasies.

"Leave her alone," my father shouted at Ziba. "You've never had eyes to see her. You're the one who drove her away from here."

"Her mother was a whore and you're still talking about her."

"Shut up or else . . ."

"I'm only telling the truth."

My father moved swiftly towards her.

She took a few steps backward and then began to

run. He ran after her, dragging his body.

Ziba went up the stairs to their bedroom and shut it from the inside. He followed her and banged on the door. "Come out right now. Don't try to hide there."

Ziba did not answer. After a moment he stopped threatening. He came back down and, without looking at me, went towards the outside door. I heard it slam shut.

Ziba came out and sat on the steps.

"I know you always hated me," she said, playing nervously with the thin gold bracelets on her wrist. She had worn those as long as I knew her. She began to cry.

"Don't cry. I'll be leaving soon."

But she kept sobbing. "I'm always going to be miserable. I'll never have peace."

Her childhood, as she had told me repeatedly, had been grim. She was forced to take care of five younger sisters and brothers while her mother worked. Her first husband, twice her age, had been abusive until he died. Then she was left with Darius to care for.

Abruptly she stopped crying and took off one of the gold bracelets and held it toward me. "Here, take this. I want you to have it."

"Thanks but I hardly ever wear jewelry. It will be wasted."

"Take it anyway, as a souvenir from me."

"If you're sure."

"I am," she said.

I took the bracelet and put it into my pocketbook, feeling it like a burden.

Outside I nearly stumbled over Darius, who was sitting

on the steps, trapping flies with his hands. "Where are you going, Feri?" he asked, looking up.

"To the passport bureau. I remember that these offices are very slow."

"Leaving already? Why do you want to run away like this? Relax, take it easy." He glanced quickly at the house down the street. "Sit down and talk to me for a while. Tell me what you've learned about life."

"I don't know. Nothing that I can report."

He followed a fly with his eyes and caught it swiftly in his hands. Holding it between two fingers, he plucked its wings and discarded its body into the gutter. "There! Flies are a curse."

Darius glanced again at the house down the street.

"Are you waiting for someone?" I asked.

He blushed. "There's a girl in that house, a beautiful girl. We write to each other all the time. I have a box full of her letters. I dream about her almost every night."

"So you're in love." I could imagine the letters—sweet and cloying and exaggerated in their expression of desire. "Are you going to marry her?"

Darius was quiet for a moment, his big shoulders hunched. "I wish I could."

"Why can't you?"

His head still bent, he said, "She isn't pure any more."

I felt embarrassed and unexpectedly hurt by the crudeness of his words. "It's your doing, I assume, that she isn't pure."

He misunderstood. "That's exactly it. How can I marry her when I know all about it?" He stared at me persistently.

"I must go now," I said.

"Why don't you wait until tomorrow. I'll take you to the passport bureau."

I shook my head. "I'd better go now."

"I'm your brother. Can't you ever listen to me?"

I shrugged and tried to smile. I wondered if he had known the truth about my mother all along.

5

I ached with memories of my mother as I walked along the narrow, dusty street to the wider one. She sits under a tree in the late afternoon, with a glow of twilight all around. A furry kitten plays with a fallen pine cone. The courtyard is very quiet except for the cooing of the pigeons or the movement of the cat.

On another afternoon my mother walks towards me in the courtyard. "Here, I made this for you," she whispers, handing me a huge rag doll. She bends down to kiss me and walks away and that is the last I see of her.

For a long time I would follow my father around and ask him over and over, "When is she coming back?" He would always say, "I don't know." He would hold me to himself and rock me, saying, "It will be all right. You have me to care for you."

I would go from room to room, looking for things that belonged to my mother. The two red felt-covered trunks where my mother kept her clothes were still there, and a pair of slippers lay beside them, heel to heel. I would touch the shoes. I opened one trunk and smelled her clothes, rubbing them against my skin. Silk scarves, velvet dresses with bright floral designs, frilly underwear scented with rosewater. All that, along with the photographs of my mother, were discarded by my father later; everything vanished, as he hoped her memory would.

After a while I threw away the rag doll she had given to me. Her absence and the rag doll had become associated, and the doll now seemed unspeakably alien.

What if my mother lived somewhere nearby? What if I could go to see her, actually talk to her after all these years?

Should I put off going to the passport bureau? No, I decided. I was afraid of being stranded here, of not being able to get out as quickly as I wanted. Years ago, when I had come to the same office, the clerk had said—and had repeated it for months—"You come back in a few days." For weeks I had been tense with frustration.

At the passport bureau I entered a hall that was crowded with people filling out forms or waiting. Clerks were busy behind a wooden counter. The air was heavy with odors of sweat and cologne. I stood on a line leading to the counter with the first letter of my last name.

"You have to leave your passport here for a while," the clerk said when it was my turn. He was a heavy, tall man with a pock-marked face. "We keep it here until we've checked into your record."

"How long would that take?"

"Oh, a few days."

"But I want to leave immediately." I knew a few days meant at least a week.

"That's how long it takes."

"But what if there's an emergency?"

"Do you have a letter from your husband, giving you permission for the trip?"

"Permission? No. I didn't know anything about that."

"We'll need that before we can give you an exit visa."

"This is ridiculous, crazy," I said.

"Step aside please so that I can help someone else," he said, not looking at me.

The young woman standing behind me tapped me on the shoulder. "That's part of the routine. I had to do that too last time I came. Ask your husband to write a letter saying that you came here with his full knowledge and permission."

Another Iranian woman standing in line leaned towards me and said quietly, "This is only the beginning of trouble. They'll make you run around for weeks. I've already been here two months longer than I intended."

"Oh, no."

"That's right. They'll find some excuse to hold you. They have nothing else to do with their time."

"But my husband is an American and I'm a resident of the United States—Americans don't write letters of permission for their wives," I said to the clerk, trying to keep hysteria out of my voice.

"Oh, you should have said so from the beginning." He picked up my passport and disappeared into a section blocked off by a curtain. He took an inordinately long time and the people in the line began to complain.

Finally he came back and said, "We have no record of your marriage."

I reached into my pocketbook and took out my marriage certificate.

"Here. It's a good thing I thought of bringing this with me."

He took the paper and looked at it for a moment. "Did you register this with the Iranian embassy?"

"I didn't know I was supposed to."

"We don't recognize this marriage," he said, becoming impatient. "It never was registered. We have no record of it."

"Of course you wouldn't have a record. Not if I didn't report it. At any rate, don't you see that I'm a resident of the United States?"

"What difference does that make?" he said. "You're still a citizen of this country. If you were married to an American . . ."

"Look at my last name here—it's an American name."

He stared at McIntosh and pronounced it a few times with the accent on the last syllable so that it almost sounded Persian. "That can be any name. Go to the office next door and tell them the situation." He looked away from me. "Next, please."

I stepped out of the line, wondering what to do. I decided to try the office he had mentioned.

I tried to look unconcerned as I stood before the man who was in charge. He was middle-aged and had dark, suspicious eyes. Another man, young and heavy set, was sitting on a chair near him and they were talking, either oblivious of or indifferent to my presence.

The man in charge suddenly turned to me and said, with an edge to his voice, "What do you want?"

I explained the problem.

"What are you bringing that problem to me for? We have more than enough work to do as it is," he said, his eyes sharply focused on me.

The other man nodded slightly in agreement and then they began to talk to each other again.

"I thought perhaps you could write a letter, telling them . . ."

"There's nothing I can do for you," he interrupted. "You have to go through the whole procedure. If anyone told you we make exceptions they're just trying to smear our name."

"But what's the procedure?"

"Go downstairs, turn right in the hall, and walk all the way to the end. There's an office there to take care of marriage certificates. Explain to them that you didn't know you were supposed to register your marriage."

"Then I won't need a letter of permission?"

"Of course you do, American husband or Iranian. It doesn't make any difference."

"Look, what's going on here? They just told me that if I'm married to an American I don't need a letter of permission."

"They must have made a mistake."

"You're a bunch of idiots who don't know what to do with your time," I said. The hysteria was all in my voice now. I went out and slammed the door.

Outside the building two men sat on the curb of the street with their legs spread, their heads tilted downward. As I got closer, I had a glimpse of what they were doing. They had unzipped their flies and were holding their penises in their hands, making a shower of urine rise into the air and then form a puddle on the ground.

I walked to another street and looked for a taxi. My head ached and my limbs felt heavy.

When the taxi pulled up before my father's house Darius was filling the bathroom pitcher with water from the pool in the courtyard. Ziba was emptying ashes out of a samovar and my father sat on the veranda, smoking a water pipe. I thought: I am here and these people, these strangers, may be my companions for a long time. What will we talk about—the next meal, how I will burn in hell for living with a man not my husband?

"Back finally!" Darius cried as though he had been waiting for me all this time. "You shouldn't wander around by yourself. Next time let me take you where you want to go."

"Come here, my daughter, and tell me what you've been doing," my father said, with no remnant of his anger.

"They're giving me trouble at the passport bureau. Can I use the phone to call Tony?" It occurred to me that I had never used his name with them before. "My husband. I'll reverse the charges."

"Go ahead, you know where the phone is," my father said. "Don't worry about reversing it—I'll pay for it."

"Thank you," I said.

He shook his head. "I'm your father."

"Do you want me to help you?" Darius asked.

"No, I can do it." I looked at my watch. It was three o'clock. About midnight in Lexington. That was a good time to call. I would be certain to get Tony at home. I went into the living room, where the telephone was, and dialed the international operator. She spoke in English and for an instant I was at a loss for words. Finally I managed to tell her the number. There was a short wait, and then she put me through.

Instead of Tony, another man answered, in a sleepy voice.

"May I speak to Tony?" I said. "This is Feri, his wife."

"Oh, hello. This is Jerry. Where *are* you?"

"I'm in Iran. Is Tony there?"

Jerry was a graduate student at the university where Tony taught.

"Sorry, Tony isn't here. He went away."

"Went away? Where to?"

"I'm not sure. I needed a place this week and he said I could stay here."

"When is he coming back?"

"In about a week. Do you want me to leave a message for him?"

"No, it's better if I call back." My father, Darius, and Ziba did not know English. If Tony called when I was out, they would not be able to take his message.

I hung up and held my head in my hands. I wanted to cry but tears would not come. A sharp pain flashed through my chest and disappeared. The pain came every so often now but had not gotten worse.

Tony had gone away without telling me. Where, I wondered. Why? Was he with someone else? A woman? Some months before, on a fall evening, we had gone to visit our friends, Julie and Kenneth. We had spent most of the evening drinking wine and smoking marijuana.

I had suggested going for a walk. We passed from street to street, pausing now and then to look at the unusual shapes of windows or the designs shadows made on a tree trunk. The air was warm, the lights blinked fuzzily.

Tony and Julie had gotten far ahead of Kenneth and me and had disappeared into another street. I was beginning to feel uncomfortable.

"I think they went that way," Kenneth said, looking uncomfortable too.

We began to walk faster, turning into a long side street and then the path off it.

I stopped for a fraction of a second before I resumed walking. Had Kenneth missed what I had seen? Had I seen anything? Later, when I went over it, turning it round and round in my head, it seemed unreal, imaginary. But at the time I thought I saw it with certainty. Underneath a large tree, near a hedge, Tony and Julie stood in an embrace, kissing. Then, as though within the same fraction of a second, they were merely standing side by side, staring at something beyond the hedge.

"Here you are," Kenneth said to them. I thought his voice was unusually loud, forced.

Julie and Tony turned and came towards us. Julie was smiling broadly.

"I think we should get going," Tony said to me.

The four of us began to walk back as if nothing had happened. But surely what I had seen underneath the branches of the tree, just a moment before, could not have been false.

In bed that night I said, "Do you like Julie now? You used to think she's too erratic."

"I like her."

"You like her a lot? I mean . . ."

"What's this cross-examining?"

"I don't know. You were talking to her for so long and so intently and . . ." I could not bring myself to make the accusation.

"She was telling me about some idea she had about people living in plastic houses—so that everything is exposed. That way we learn not to be ashamed of anything."

Tony yawned.

That was the beginning of my suspicions of his infidelities, sometimes confirmed, sometimes unproven.

The beginning also of my own infidelities.

My father and Darius had come into the room and were looking at me. I was standing by the phone, as if I were paralyzed.

"What happened?" my father asked.

"He wasn't in. He has gone away for a week."

"There's no rush for you to go back. If you return so quickly he won't appreciate you. What does a man think of a woman with no sense of family?" Darius said.

"I'm tired. I'd like to rest," I said.

"Maybe you weren't so happy there," my father said. "Or else why come back now, after so many years?"

I went to my room and sat on the bed and tried to think of what to do next. There was not much I could do. I had to wait until I reached Tony. In a way I was more anxious than before to get back, to settle things with Tony—the memory of the walk that night tormented me even more acutely now than when it had occurred. But I was not sure what I would say to him—he resisted talks.

The sense of helplessness I had felt since I came on the visit began to envelop me. As the afternoon darkened to twilight, I seemed to go back to my childhood, to the time when my mother left. Waiting and waiting for her and she never returning.

I remember seeing a square figure, wrapped in a *chador*, standing at the darkened end of the street, signalling to me to come out. I feel a thrill, an electric connection with that figure and run out into the street. I run with extraordinary speed. I come to a sudden stop before the figure, my mother. Inch by inch I am buried farther under her *chador*, hidden, safe, and at this point I begin to cry. I feel the muscles of her stomach twitching under my chin, shaking with fear, joy? She lays her head on my shoulder and mutters, "They won't let me see you, they won't let me. One day I'm going to come and take you away. Yes, one day. . . ." I am aware of the fabric of her dress on my cheek, silky, slippery. After that, every afternoon, I stand by the window, waiting for her.

At times I was afraid of seeing her again. Perhaps she was angry at something I had done and that was why she had gone away, or perhaps she would be monstrously changed into someone I could not recognize.

Then I thought, my father—others I loved—could disappear too, for no reason I would understand. Suddenly, without notice. I asked my father over and over, "Will you always stay with me?"

"Of course, of course," he would say at first, reassuringly.

But finally my question became a nuisance, an obvious and ugly compulsion, like a tic. To make me stop, my father resorted to punishment. He hit me on the bottom with a dry branch. "Are you going to say that again, are you?" he asked with each blow. When I rose, sobbing, I saw his face flushed and twitching. He panted heavily. The punishment silenced me but I developed a dry, monotonous cough. My father again tried to stop me, this time in a different way. One with a white liquid and said, "I got this for you from the doctor. Take two tablespoons each time you cough." I followed his instructions and the cough disappeared after a

while. A few years later he told me that the liquid was just
sugar water.

6

If only I could see my mother and talk to her, I thought. Maybe my cousin Simin could tell me something about her whereabouts.

The sky outside had turned to a deep gray where one star blinked. A few mosquitoes buzzed near the window. I slipped from my room and started for Simin's house. The streets were awake and noisy. Young boys stood on street corners, talking. Music flowed out of cinemas. I zigzagged rapidly through the streets, somewhat calmed by the activity and the cool night air.

Lights winked like a row of yellow stars along Molavi Street, where Simin lived. Except for a small grocery store with several customers in it, the street was quiet and empty.

I knocked at Simin's door and after a few moments it was opened. In the dim light I saw a little girl grinning at me. Her face was flat and unnaturally large with beady black eyes. From her small round shoulders, which were almost the continuation of a thick neck, two folds of flesh hung, instead of arms. She had an enlarged belly and tiny legs.

"Is Simin in? I'm her cousin, Feri."

The folds of flesh on the little girl's shoulders began to sway back and forth like fins as she said in a high, tinny voice, "I've heard so much about you. My mother talks about you all the time."

My father had written something to me about this child, the victim of a drug Simin took during her pregnancy—thalidomide probably. At first, he wrote, the deformity had caused a lot of talk among the neighbors. It was God's punishment for some sin, they said.

I followed the child into a small courtyard. In some spots the cement had cracked. Simin and two young girls sat on a rug eating watermelon. An old man leaned against the wall, puffing at a water pipe. They all looked sallow under a shadeless bulb hanging on the wall. There was a commotion as I walked in.

"What a nice surprise," Simin said, getting up and embracing me. Then we sat on the rug. She introduced the girl who had opened the door to me as Zizi and the other two as Maryam and Ziba. She said her two sons were not home at the moment. Zizi smiled, blushed at the introduction, and her body jerked slightly. The other two were docile and quiet, and soon they got up and went inside.

Simin's husband stared at me, dipped his head imperceptibly, and said, "It's nice of you to pay us a visit." Then he sank back into himself, puffing at the water pipe. I pictured him as he was years before when he sat on his wedding chair beside Simin. He had been old then too with all his thoughts submerged in the back of his eyes. Only now his eyes were more vacant.

"Maryam will be getting married soon," Simin said.

"But she's so young," I protested.

"How can I refuse a husband for her? Anyway, fifteen is not that young. I was about that age when I got married."

I could hear a radio playing soft, mournful Persian

music. Simin filled a plate with slices of watermelon and put it before me. Zizi sat beside her father, leaning her head on his arm.

"Zizi can read and write. She's very smart. She went to school for a few years," Simin said.

"I like school," Zizi said.

"Why haven't you had any children?" Simin asked me. "It's not natural to be married and have no children."

"I had a miscarriage and after that I didn't want to have a child. The desire disappeared."

"I couldn't conceive of living without my children. I'd feel dead, useless without them. Tell me, how do you spend your time every day?"

"I work. That takes most of my time."

"Do you have someone to help you with the housework?"

"No, but I don't have much housework. A lot of things are automatic in America, easier to do than here."

"How nice that must be. But how do you feel living in a foreign land, without your family?" She assessed me carefully for the first time. "You've changed—you've become Western."

"How have I changed?"

She looked thoughtful, not quite listening to me. "It must have been like hermits who go into a cave to try to forget their other lives. . . . Remember how close you and I were?"

"Yes, we were together all the time." Simin had been bouncy and robust and I helplessly shy. We would play hide-and-seek and later, when older, we would talk and talk in the darkened courtyard, lit only by the flicker of a pressure lamp, or on a roof beneath stars. Then Simin was suddenly grown, about to get married.

The night before the wedding we stayed up all night, whispering, confiding. "I feel closer to you than to anyone else in the world," Simin had said. "Nothing is going to make us grow apart, not marriage, not having children."

On the wedding night Simin sat smiling behind the gauzy veil of her wedding dress, two orange and yellow glass bracelets glimmering on her wrist. She seemed to blend with the glow of colors and noise all about—the exquisite platters of fruit and saffron rice, bouquets of flowers, patches of sequins on the guests' dresses, rows of pearls and gold jewelry, sounds of laughter, admiration and concern. Older members of the family, sitting in a corner and fanning themselves, were already whispering about the flaws in the bridegroom's character—he had been ungenerous in his gifts to the bride, he rarely spoke or smiled.

I thought of my own wedding, standing beside Tony in a simple white dress in the City Hall. I had felt a remoteness from everything around me—the cream-colored walls, the dark heavy doors and furniture, the clerk himself. I had looked up at Tony and felt like giggling.

We had married there and then we had gone for a week's honeymoon to Nantucket. We bicycled all over the small island, ate in quiet restaurants overlooking the sea, made love at all times of the day and stayed up late at night to read aloud to each other.

Zizi yawned loudly.

"Why don't you go inside, dear, where your sisters are," Simin suggested.

Zizi's head moved back and forth and finally she fixed

her eyes on her mother. "They only talk with each other."

"Oh, are you feeling sad, dear? Come here, let me kiss you. You'll feel better."

Zizi sat on her mother's lap, putting a hand on her breast.

"Pretty soon your own breasts will grow," Simin said. "Right here." She brushed her hand over Zizi's chest. "Two little breasts. You're only eleven—maybe in a year or two."

"Will I look like you then?"

"Sure." She put her fingers into Zizi's curls. "You're my nicest girl."

Zizi yawned again. "I'm going to sleep."

"I have to help her get undressed," Simin explained. "I'll be right out." She went with Zizi.

Simin's husband had fallen asleep with his head against the wall, snoring. I watched a row of ants going towards an empty flower bed. The shadows swam with them. When Simin returned she woke her husband. "Why don't you go in? You fell asleep."

He stared at Simin for a moment and got up without saying a word.

Simin watched him go inside and then said, "I wonder where his mind is all the time."

"He's just a quiet person," I said.

"He should never have gotten married."

I shrugged, thinking of what Tony's mother had once said about him. "I'm so glad he met you. I worried sometimes if he'd ever settle down. On every holiday he brought another girl home." At another time Tony said to me, "With you I don't feel that marriage is a burden. You know how to leave me alone."

Now I wondered if we had left each other alone too much.

"His sisters wanted him to marry, so he did," Simin was saying. She sighed. "They picked me, probably because they thought he would never get attached to me. Or maybe because he's incapable of getting attached to anyone. His parents died when he was very young and those sisters hovered over him and cared for him. They're the only people who matter to him."

"I remember how you cried and pleaded with your mother not to force you to marry him." Was I much happier for having selected Tony?

"I've wasted my life on him. And now my daughter is getting married and I have to spend every moment of my time preparing a dowry for her. I have no time for anything else and the worry is wearing me out."

"Why don't you buy some things ready made?"

"That takes money, you know." Tears filled Simin's eyes.

"How much money would you need?"

"No less than a thousand *tomans*. It's not easy to get together so much when you have five children—all needing to be fed and clothed."

A thousand *tomans* was a little more than a hundred dollars.

"It eats my heart out the way my daughter tries to comfort me. 'Don't worry mother. If we're patient, God will help us out,' she says to me. And her fiance is so young and sweet. . . ." She began to cry, tears pouring from her eyes.

"Don't worry. I can give you some money. I brought more with me than I can spend."

Simin continued crying. "And Zahara is fourteen. Soon she'll be the age to be married and my worries will start all over again."

"Here, I'll give you the money right now." I reached for my pocketbook and took out a stack of bills. "Here, take this."

Simin stretched her hands and enfolded the money in them quickly. "I'm grateful to you for this. I'll never forget your kindness." There was no trace of embarrassment in her voice. Her whole face and tone reflected infinite relief. She folded the bills and lay them under the handle of a knife.

"Did I tell you how miserable your father was because you didn't write? Sometimes he'd start crying at the mention of your name."

"You said something about that."

"In a way I don't blame you for not wanting to come back here. Life must be so much easier for you there."

I groped for a way to bring up the subject of my mother.

"Remember my mother used to take us on the train to Shah-Abdol-Azim?" I said.

"Yes, of course. We did so much together."

"You and I would stand by the window and wait for the blue domes. There were all those wild flowers on the roads and the goats and cows, and peasants selling rag dolls." I could see the antiquated train with its rickety benches, soot-covered walls, and the black plume of smoke swarming and swirling around it.

"Once she bought each of us a pinwheel," Simin said. "You broke yours and kept crying and we couldn't find another one to buy for you so I purposely broke mine. That only made you cry harder."

"Do you know where she's living right now?" I hesitated and then went on. "My father told me that she had left him for another man."

I could see contradictory emotions playing on Simin's face. "I guess she did," she said finally, her hands fidgeting over the fraying edge of the rug. "I don't know where she is."

I could taste my disappointment. "It doesn't make sense that I wasn't allowed to see her, or live with her part of the time."

"I guess because of this other man. . . ."

"Can you really blame my mother for wanting to follow her feelings? It must have been a strong passion, devastating, for her to abandon everything, even her child."

Simin bit her lips, lowered her eyes, and all she could say was, "May God forgive her for her sins."

"Who was this other man anyway?"

"A young, handsome man who had worked in her father's office and later, for a while, for your father. He was an accountant or something." She rubbed her fingers on a stain on her blouse. "You became shy after she left."

"I guess I was ashamed. I thought it could be my fault that she left, or that others would think it was my fault."

Simin nodded.

"I wish I could see a picture of her," I said.

"I may have one among the old pictures. I can go and see."

She went inside again and I waited. When she came out carrying a bag full of photographs, I took them and looked at them one by one. Some were group or individual family pictures and some were just scenes—a cliff, a mountain, a particularly dramatic mass of clouds.

Simin pointed to two photographs, both of the same woman. "These are your mother."

I looked at them closely. She was young and beautiful but her expression was quite different in the two pictures. In one she held onto the column of a porch, her head tilted back, laughing. The wind played in her heavy, coiling hair, making it whip around her face and neck. She seemed extremely happy at first glance, but as I looked more carefully I saw that her eyes were haunted, frightened.

In the other picture she sat on a rug, her legs stretched out, a book open on her lap. She wore a *chador*, covering most of her hair, and her eyes and face were expressionless. It was impossible to tell what emotion lay behind that mask of detachment.

My eyes filled with tears. "I couldn't remember her face that well," I said.

"Supposedly she was the prettiest girl on her street. She had many suitors but your grandparents selected your father for her. They said he had a head on his shoulders. I think they thought your father was wealthier than he was." Her voice seemed to hang in the air. And then it was as if she was talking to herself. "I used to be pretty, too, remember? Now look at me. I'm a bag of sticks and bones."

I remembered Simin's glowing face behind the white organdy of her wedding gown. And again my own face held up towards Tony.

"Do you have any idea how I can find out more about my mother?" I asked. "Please. Anything."

"Let me think." She closed her eyes for a minute. "She has an old relative, Zeinab Dashti, who lives on Kgani Abad

Street. Her house is on the right-hand side all the way at the end of the street. She might know where your mother is."

"I'm going to go and see her."

"It would be so exciting if you really did find your mother."

"In a way I can't imagine it. It all seems incredible." But I felt excitement rising in me.

As soon as I returned from Simin's house, I took two aspirins and went to bed. The pain in my body had started up again. I still had not developed fever. Perhaps there was something wrong with my heart. But I discarded that idea since the pain travelled up and down sporadically, latching itself to various spots. I would give it a few more days and then consult a doctor, I resolved, trying to relax, to put myself to sleep.

Every time I woke during the night I realized I had dreamed about my mother, dreams that had shaken me out of sleep but whose content I did not recall. I remembered one dream I had near dawn. I was standing by the door of the house, when I saw my mother coming towards me, her arms held by two other women. They all walked with their heads down. My mother seemed to be resisting and the two women were dragging her. Then she suddenly looked up. As soon as she saw me she began to scream and run the other way.

In the morning I took a taxi to Kgani Abad, a long, narrow street in an old, far-off section of the city. The cobblestoned sidewalks were full of rubbish and dried-up spittle. Some women were washing clothes in the dirty water of the gutter. They lifted their heads and stared at me in my short dress.

A little boy, his belly enlarged, stood by the steps of a dilapidated shrine. He stretched one hand towards me, and said, "Give me a *rial*, please give me a *rial.*" A man with an amputated leg, a woman, and then another little boy joined in, all asking for money. I gave each two *rials* and walked away. As I looked down the street I almost expected to see my mother waiting. She used to sit with her knees drawn up against her chest when my father or I was late coming home. The edge of her *chador* would be wet and full of holes, where she had chewed on it.

At the end of the street I found the house and knocked a few times. Soon I could hear footsteps approaching. An old women, erect, pale, with sharp, dark eyes and wearing a *chador*, opened the door to me.

"Are you Zienab *Khanom?*" I asked.

"Yes," she said.

"I'm looking for Banoo *Khanom*. I wonder if you could tell me where she lives."

"She doesn't live in Teheran any more." She stared at me with curiosity. "She's been living in Kashan for years."

"Do you have her address? I'm her daughter."

She looked confused for an instant and then said excitedly, "Her daughter! My god, you must be Feri."

"I've been away for many years."

"You wouldn't remember me. You were very little when your mother brought you here for visits. Come in, come in now."

I followed her into the hallway. She hugged and kissed me and said, "I can't believe it! After all these years!"

We went to the courtyard which was small and shaded by overgrown trees. A worn-out rug was spread by a pool of water. Melon seeds and bits of bread lay scattered on the ground. She pointed to me to sit on the rug, then went down into a basement and came back with a samovar, a tea pot and two glasses. The samovar was already lit. She filled the tea pot with hot water from the samovar and set it on top to heat. Then she sat also, her legs crossed, her hands folded on her lap. A young girl opened the doors of a room, looked at me with curiosity and shut the doors again. A small child, sucking on a pacifier, stood in a doorway of another room, staring at me.

"Once your mother brought you here and you kept running around, trying to catch a bird. You were stung by a bee. Your mother held your finger and sucked it where it had been stung," Zeinab said.

"What's she doing in Kashan?" I knew Kashan was an ancient town with ruins and clay houses.

"It was her fate to get stranded in a strange city, away from her relatives. But luckily her brother is with her. Do you remember your uncle Mohammed?"

"Yes," I said, "Vaguely."

She reached out and touched my cheek. "You must have gone through so much but your poor mother did too. She used to go back to your house, hoping to have a glimpse of you. Then she came here and stayed with me for a while and all she talked about was how she wanted to die. She would open the door to the cistern and sit at the edge. I would have to go and pull her out. Finally I had to put a lock on that door."

"Wasn't she happy with him, that man?"

"Happy? How could she—having lost you, her only child? Besides he always reminded her that once she had been another man's wife."

"What happened to him?"

67

"He stayed with her for a while and then disappeared. Just as your mother was beginning to get used to that, he came back again and talked her into selling a house she had in her name and going to Kashan with him. He opened a bakery there with that money, sold the bakery after a while, and went away with the money."

"Then how has she been supporting herself?"

"She's been managing somehow. I think your uncle had some money." She started to pour tea into the glasses.

"Thank you, I don't want any tea," I said. It seemed I would choke if I tried to drink it. "But I wonder if you could give me her address."

7

My father was sitting in the living room, reading a newspaper.

"I'm going to Kashan. My mother lives there."

"What?" He looked astounded by my abrupt news. "Who told you that? How do you know it's true?"

"It's true. I talked to one of her relatives."

"Is that what you've been doing running around?" he said indignantly. "Why didn't you tell me about it? Why don't you ever tell me anything?"

"I'm sorry. I just found out yesterday."

"What's everyone going to think?"

"Can't you try to understand . . ." I fumbled for words. "It's natural for me to want to see her?"

"Was it natural for her to leave you?" He got up and came towards me rapidly as if my words had filled him with too much energy.

"You stopped her from seeing me," I said, immediately regretting it. He looked so desperate standing there before me, trying to block my way. "Anyway, it doesn't matter."

"I stopped her because I didn't want her to contaminate you."

I forced myself into silence.

"You're not going to see her," he said.

I began to walk away.

He grabbed my arm. "Go back into that room and stay there."

"No," I said, pulling away.

He dropped his hand to his side, his whole body slackening suddenly. "Go then, get out of my sight."

"I won't stay long," I said, trying to keep my voice level.

I took a taxi to the bus terminal, bought a ticket and got on the bus immediately. I wanted to be sure of a seat by the window.

The roads were narrow and curving, weaving through a vast desert. The color all around was a whitish-gray—the sand, the salt lakes, and the sky blending. Here and there I saw stubby trees, the ruins of inns and old villages.

The bus was filled to its capacity with passengers and luggage piled on the racks, under the seats, the aisle. People talked loudly or whispered to each other, the voices going on and on, mingling with the screech of the tires against the roadway. Children sucked on sweets, ate watermelon seeds and threw the shells on the floor, or sat silently looking out of the windows. Occasionally they cried or screamed or laughed.

Next to me sat an old woman who immediately put her head back and fell asleep. I tried to sleep too but the bus, jarring against bumps on the road, kept me awake. The excitement I felt at the prospect of seeing my mother paled gradually as people turned to look at me and whispered to each other. I was the only woman on the bus not wearing a *chador* and the only woman travelling alone. And what bond really existed between my mother and me at this point?

I could see the bus driver staring at me in the mirror. He smiled. His teeth were surprisingly white and even.

I closed my eyes to avoid him and this time fell asleep.

When I woke we were passing through Khom, a religious town, filled with women shrouded in dark *chadors* and men wearing *abas*.

Golden domes glistened in the sun. A row of cars covered with black cloths and adorned with flowers passed by —a funeral. I recalled a saying about Khom, "They import the dead and export priests."

The bus stopped for gas just outside of Khom and the passengers began to get out. We had one hour to rest and I wondered what to do with myself.

I got out of the bus and passed a huge restaurant, where many people were sitting having tea or eating, smoking cigarettes or water pipes. It was noisy, dirty, and unappetizing. I went to the back, where the restrooms were. I used the toilet with reluctance. It was so dirty and had such a strong stench.

Then I went into the bazaar across from the station. I walked around for a while. Little boys and girls leaned against walls or walked about idly. Some of them began to follow me, just watching me.

The shopkeepers sipped tea, passed rosaries between their fingers, banged with hammers against metal or stared into space, their faces immobile, their bodies limp. An old man held up a necklace, urging me to buy it. He smiled and smiled, looking a little crazy. Another old man, lining copper items with a thin layer of tin, beckoned to me to see his goods. I bought a copper colander and a mortar and pestle at prices incredibly low, even by Iranian standards. Then I bought a skewer of *kebab* and a glass of *doogh* from a stall and ate them.

As I walked back I felt something brushing against me, on and off, persistently. I turned around. It was a young man. He winked at me. I kept all expression out of my face and walked on towards the bus rapidly.

The bus arrived in Kashan two hours later than scheduled, having taken eight hours. I was aching all over, and my hair was covered with a layer of dust.

It was dusk and the air was drier and considerably warmer than it had been in Teheran.

I took one of the taxis lined up by the station and gave the driver my mother's address. We passed a cluster of mud houses, a square, and a wide street, lined with more elegant houses.

Then we entered an older section, where many houses were only partially intact. Most of them had domes and windtowers on the roofs to keep the inside cool. The driver stopped by a narrow lane. Surrounded by mud and straw walls, it looked like a tunnel. The house stood all by itself inside an alley off the lane. I paid the driver and got out.

I knocked on the door of the house several times and waited. Did my mother really live here? How would she react to me, a stranger, suddenly turning up and claiming to be her daughter? A sense of the absurdity of the trip struck me. But the next instant I pictured my mother squatting in the shade of a tree, washing clothes in abundant suds or walking around with a broom sweeping dry leaves and twigs from rose bushes. Seeing me she pauses and we look at each other, first like strangers and then our faces form into familiar shapes, shining over the expanse of years. "It's me, Feri," I say. "I know, I know," she says. We embrace, our faces full of tears.

No one answered the knocks. I put my head against the door and listened but there were no sounds from the inside. I went back into the lane and looked around, hoping to spot someone who would tell me whether my mother still lived there. Several boys sat in the dust, playing with rounded little rocks, their bare legs spread open, not bothering to wave away the flies swimming around their eyes.

A little girl came out of a house and began to stare at me. "You should go to the Bagh Fin," she said. "That's where all the tourists go."

"Do you know Banoo *Khanom?*" I asked.

"Yes, she lives right there."

"Do you know where she is right now? She doesn't seem to be home."

"No." She shrugged. "I can show you around if you want. I know every place in this town."

"Maybe later."

I went back and knocked at the door again. Still there was no answer. Uncertain, I waited for a while and then decided to check into a hotel and come back in the morning.

I walked to the wider street and waited for a taxi. Many cabs went by ignoring my raised hand and finally one stopped. "Parsi Inn," I said to the driver, having seen that name on the way.

The corridor of the hotel had a foul smell. It was lit by a naked bulb, around which mosquitoes hummed. A man was sitting behind a desk and an older man was rising and reclining over a prayer rug in a corner.

"Do you have any single rooms?" I asked the man behind the desk.

"Are you by yourself?" He had deep-set black eyes and wore an old suit which hung loosely on him.

I thought I caught a hint of suspicion in his eyes and was afraid again of being a woman alone in that backward, religious town. "Yes," I said hesitantly.

He pointed to the man praying. "He's the boss. We'll have to wait until he's finished."

Soon the man finished praying and came towards us, his eyes turned downward. "I wish women wouldn't go around without *chadors*. This town is being infested by them." He had a goiter under his chin and he kept drawing in his mucous and swallowing it.

I thought of leaving and going to another hotel but I felt exhausted from the bus ride and was not sure what the other hotels would be like.

"She wants a room. Do we have any left?" the younger man asked him.

He did not reply for a moment, then turning his back to me, he whispered something to the younger man. The other man whispered back. Then the older man said, "We've only one room left, a good one overlooking the garden for 110 *tomans*. I can show it to you if you want.

The sum, about $16, seemed outrageous for that dismal hotel but I said, "Fine, I'll take it."

"Sit over there and wait. I'll make a bed for you," the man behind the desk said.

I sat on a chair and waited, waving away mosquitoes. There was no sign of life in the corridor and I was sure that most of the rooms were unoccupied. I felt relieved when a young man and a woman came along the corridor and went

74

into one of the rooms.

The man returned. "You can go into the room now," he said.

"Is it possible to have food sent into my room?" I asked.

"I can get you something from the restaurant next door."

"Would you get me chicken and a coke?"

"All right." He accompanied me to the room, carrying my valise. Then he left.

The room was small and painted green. There was a cot in a corner, with a bright pink imitation velvet bedspread. A fake leopardskin rug covered the floor next to the bed and an earthen pitcher of water stood on the window sill.

I went to the window, pulled open the gauze curtains and looked out. All I could see were the mass of trees and stars flaring in the sky.

I turned and sat at the edge of the bed, mechanically brushing away mosquitoes which kept attacking my neck, face, arms. Somewhere a radio went on and a high voice carried on a slow, mournful melody. There was a tap-tap of footsteps in the corridor, starting and stopping.

Suddenly I became aware of a tiny black bug crawling on the bedspread. I looked closely—it was a tick. I jumped up and pulled off the bedspread and inspected the sheets underneath. They were a bluish color from bleach and seemed clean.

I heard a knock at the door and the hotel clerk walked in with a tray of food. He put the food on the bed and lingered.

"Would you put the cost on my hotel bill?" I said.

"Yes," he said, waiting still.

I took out a bill to give to him as a tip. He took it, examined it, and stretched out his hand towards me again as though about to give the money back. "That's all?" he said. "If it hadn't been for me the boss wouldn't have let you stay here."

I took out another bill and gave it to him.

He folded the bills, put them in his pocket, and left.

The chain swung against the door. I got up and put the chain in the latch.

Then I began to eat. The food was appetizing with its lemon and mint flavor and for the first time all day I felt somewhat relaxed.

It was ten o'clock when I turned off the light and lay in bed. I woke once to what I thought was a knock at the door and I leaped up, pulled the sheet up to my chest and listened. I could hear nothing except the bark of faraway dogs and the singing of cicadas.

8

A ray of sunlight shone on the leopardskin rug when I opened my eyes in the morning. I dressed, put back my nightgown and a few other items in the valise and went to the desk. I paid and left quickly.

Outside, in the stalls, in open cafes, and on sidewalks, men sipped tea or smoked water pipes. By daylight the streets suggested languor rather than threat. All my tensions and fears disappeared. How gentle and harmless everyone seemed, how indifferent to my existence. I paused by a stall where hot beets and milk were sold and had some of each.

Then I took a taxi to my mother's address. This time the door was open but a heavy cloth blocked the view inside. I knocked on the open door. Again there was no answer. I pushed the cloth aside, entered a hallway and called, "Is anyone in?" No one answered. I went out, thinking she could not be too far.

I walked for a while through the maze of lanes and then climbed the stairway to the roof of a house that had nearly collapsed. I looked at a wide expanse of the town enveloped in early morning silence—the cupolas, the windtowers.

"You'd better come down. It's dangerous up there," said a woman from below. She was old and wore a polka dot *chador,* greasy strands of hair showed on her forehead. "Just the other day another tourist was up on a roof and it crumbled beneath him. Come down, come down." She waved her hands in alarm.

I came down.

"Many visitors come and go in this town—mostly from other countries—some of them know Farsi." She looked at me intensely, assessing me. "But you are Iranian."

"Yes," I said. "I'm looking for Banoo *Khanom* but she isn't home. Do you by chance know her?"

"Of course. She can't be too far. Maybe she went to the bazaar."

"So she should be back soon," I said.

"How do you know her?"

"I'm related to her," I said.

"Maybe her brother is home."

"No one was there just a minute ago."

"If you like, I'll show you Mr. Boroojerdi's house while you're waiting. All tourists look at it."

I followed the woman through several streets. She took me inside a house with an immense courtyard and old cypress trees. We climbed up a flight of stairs to a porch and went into a complex of rooms. I looked at the fading friezes, inlays, and murals on the walls and ceilings.

"It took fifteen years to build this house. Mr. Boroojerdi and his family lived here. During the day the women would sit in these rooms and weave rugs. On hot days they would bathe in that pool, cool off and start all over again," the woman said. "At night they would play music, and sing and dance."

"Did you know them?" I asked.

She nodded; her dark eyes became opaque. "Yes, I visited here often. Sometimes I stayed for weeks. It was a beautiful house. They were great people. Now I live in that room and take care of the house."

I looked towards the squalid room, separate from the complex of rooms, on the other side of the courtyard. A woman and two little boys pushed aside a dark, dusty cloth hanging on its doorway and sat on the steps below.

"That's my sister and the two boys are my nephews," the woman said. "We all live here. Both of our husbands are dead."

"It must be lonely," I said.

"There are many others like us, living in houses like this, taking care of them. Banoo *Khanom* and her brother do the same thing. There's a house over there with mirrored walls. If you like I'll take you to it."

"Maybe some other time," I said, heat rising in my face at the thought of my mother being a caretaker of a similar house.

As I was leaving I tried to give a tip to the woman. She shook her head. "God bless you, but no, no. Mr. Boroojerdi was my uncle, a dear uncle."

I looked at her, puzzled.

"When he died his fortune melted like a candle. He had one son who blew away his money." She shook her head, the wrinkles on her face deepening. "It takes only one weed to choke a garden."

She went towards her sister and nephews and I left.

When I got back a man was squatting by my mother's door, staring at the palm of his hand. A stick leaned against the wall behind him. He was middle-aged and wore frayed and unpressed trousers and shirt. He had a trim face and fine features and a graying, pointed beard. I wondered if he was my uncle.

"Is Banoo *Khanom* in?" I asked. "I came here before and she was gone."

He looked up but his eyes passed mine, focusing somewhere in space.

"Yes, she's in," he said, lowering his head again.

There was something peculiar about his motions and it struck me that he was blind.

"Are you her brother?" I asked.

He nodded. I hesitated, wondering whether I should tell him who I was. He seemed part of the anonymous mass of dark figures all around. The idea of his being my uncle was totally absurd. You can still go back, I thought. Turn around and go. Quickly. But the presence of the blind man was too powerful, pulling at me, holding me.

"I'm Feri, Banoo *Khanom*'s daughter. Do you remember me?" I said. "You're uncle Mohammed, aren't you?"

He lifted his face, his expression changing into—I was not sure what—bewilderment? For a moment I was aware of an utter silence and blankness before he said, very softly, "Feri!" He did not ask any questions. Instead he got up, flung his arms around me, and put his mouth to my forehead. A vague recollection of him came to me—putting me on his shoulder when I was a child, and going round and round until I started screaming with dizziness.

He drew back and I said, "I came here last night but no one was home. So I stayed in a hotel."

"You must have come when we were at the mosque," he said. "Let me take you inside."

He picked up his stick and we went into the hall, passed

an arched, low doorway, and entered a courtyard. I felt the sun behind me. It made my head burn, seem enormous and heavy.

He walked a little ahead of me, tapping his staff against the ground, finding his way. We passed through the courtyard, another hallway, and entered a smaller courtyard. The many doors around the courtyard were open, revealing empty rooms. One of the rooms did not have a roof and a twisted tree had grown inside of it.

As we climbed some stairs, it occurred to me how silent we had been and I asked, "Is she here?"

"She was here just before." There was a dryness in his tone as though he had forgotten the surprise of my presence.

The room had white-washed walls, cracked in one place, and its only furnishings were several faded rugs. I noticed a woman sleeping on a mattress in a corner. She lay there, old, fat, her skin unnaturally sallow, her fingers and feet bloated.

"Banoo, Banoo, get up," my uncle said and my mother sat up abruptly, her bloodshot eyes focused on him, then on me, uncomprehendingly.

I knew this was a moment that I should savor, a moment that would never repeat itself. And I knew there was a right emotion that I must feel, a right gesture I could make. But I stood there motionless, feeling nothing but a weight within me.

"You'd never believe it," my uncle said to her. "This is Feri."

"Feri?" my mother said, not making the slightest movement of recognition.

"Feri, your daughter," my uncle said, and now he had that lingering smile on his face again, a smile that did not seem connected with anything.

"Feri!" I heard my mother's voice echo this time as though it were coming from a much farther distance than the few feet between us. "My God, Feri!"

"I was away . . . then I heard about you. . . ."

She had gotten up and her face was flushed, her eyes fully focused on me with some kind of delirium. "I couldn't sleep well last night. I was full of strange dreams that would wake me up, frightening dreams that I'd forget instantly."

"Maybe somewhere inside you there was an inkling of her coming," my uncle said. "I felt an expectation in me also. That's why I was sitting there by the door waiting instead of going to the Square. I was not completely surprised when she appeared there, telling me she's Feri."

I reached out and embraced my mother, hiding my face on her chest. Then, when I could no longer see her, but could feel her chest and hear her heartbeats, I had a sudden sensation that I was years back in time with no space in between, no incident to mask the startling clarity. This was my mother with the same touch, the same voice.

We sat on a rug in the courtyard and talked while waiting for lunch which was cooking in a blackened pot on a portable stove. My uncle had filled the pot with water from the pool faucet and my mother had added beans, vegetables, and homemade noodles, taking them out of small sacks. The air was extraordinarily clear and smelled of the soup cooking and spearmint growing somewhere in the courtyard.

I gave my mother and uncle a summary of my life over the last two decades, thinking how flat the bumps of incidents had grown, how drained of significance. Their account of their lives was even more faded, uttered in quieter, more hesitant tones. Was it possible to close the gap that time had created between us, I wondered in despair.

Our conversation was like a conversation in dreams, rapid, shadowy one moment and extraordinarily vivid the next.

"Yes, I lay flat for hours and hours on my back because the world had become black, completely black," my uncle would say.

"I'd hold a colorful string before you, swaying it back and forth, like Feri used to do to a cat." My mother said, laughing, showing her blackened molars.

"When I got there I realized I didn't know my way back. I don't have a good sense of direction," I said.

As in dreams, some of the connections were missing.

"Nothing in life is quite expected," my uncle said more firmly. "Who knew that I was going to lose my sight, that my sister would lose all her fortune and we'd end up in this ruined place? Yet one mustn't question God's will. Who knows why He chooses these certain paths for his creations?" Flies crawled on his beard, buzzing, climbing on each other and separating with frantic intensity. "Banoo kept questioning her lot and got herself deeper and deeper in trouble. You were lucky you didn't see her in those days when she lost her head and hid herself in a basement, too ashamed to be seen by anyone, or tried to drown herself in the cistern."

"Fate," my mother said simply. She took the lid off the pot, mixed the soup with a ladle, and began to serve it in blue ceramic bowls. Then she took out some bread folded inside of a tin box and put it before us.

"We don't have much around the house today," she said, smiling feebly. She seemed to be trying to overcome a deadly fatigue. "But later I'll get you things I know you'd like."

"Don't worry about it." I smiled too, with difficulty.

We began to eat. My uncle's eyes lay on me, perhaps unintentionally, as he dipped bread in the soup and ate it. Small, hard-shelled insects lay on their backs on the ground, their legs twitching in the air.

A sharp pain shot in my chest and began to travel around my rib cage.

"I think I'm going to lie down for a while. I'm very tired." I knew by now I should contact a doctor but I was ashamed of saying that to my mother so soon after I had arrived.

We went inside and my mother took out a mattress, some sheets and a pillow from a closet. Together we spread the mattress on the floor.

"Rest now. You've had a long trip," she said.

"Can I have something heavier than that sheet?" I asked. "I'm a little chilly."

The room was cool with the breeze coming through a wind tower on the roof but the chill I felt seemed to go beyond that. She gave me a comforter and I lay under it. Then she left the room. I fell in and out of sleep.

I could hear footsteps of people coming into the room and leaving, voices in the courtyard. I heard my uncle saying to someone. "Do you know how important it is for my sister to have her daughter here? Actually have her right in this house?"

"Important," I said the word to myself. "Important."

Then it was dark and the pain convulsed the muscles of my back, stomach, and chest. I sat up and looked around. There was no one in the room. I got out of the bed and stood by the doorway. My mother and uncle were sleeping in the courtyard on mattresses spread on rugs. The sky was bright with masses of stars and a crescent moon. Every flower, every leaf was sharply delineated. I began to pace the room. Finally I went out and kneeled beside my mother.

"Mother," I called.

She woke instantly and sat up. "What's the matter?"

"I don't feel well. I'm in pain all over."

"What? Where does it hurt exactly?"

I tried to put my hand on the places but the pain was elusive.

My uncle sat up, awakened by our voices. "Is something wrong?"

"She says she's in pain. We'd better get the doctor."

"Would a doctor come here in the middle of the night?" I asked.

"Of course," my mother said. "He's a very good doctor. He was in the United States, became a doctor there."

"Oh," I said, somewhat relieved.

"I'll walk over and get him," my uncle said. "Let me get dressed first."

He walked to the room, his motions fluid in the moonlight. He came out dressed and carrying his cane. "I'll be back soon. The doctor lives about ten streets away."

"Go back inside and rest now until the doctor comes," my mother said to me.

9

I opened my eyes to the flicker of an oil lamp. My mother and uncle and a young man were sitting beside me.

"This is Dr. Mahmood Majid," my uncle said.

The doctor and I nodded at each other.

He was thin and dark, with lively black eyes and a full beard. He looked at once alert and ascetic. He reminded me of students on Harvard Square trying to look Eastern. I stared at him, unprepared for his appearance. I had expected him to be stuffy-looking.

"I'm sorry you had to come in the middle of the night."

"Never mind." He sounded rather brusque. "Tell me, where does it hurt?"

I described the pain.

"How long have you had it?"

"Since I came to Iran—over a week ago—but it has gotten worse."

"You waited that long to see a doctor?"

"I had no fever so I thought it couldn't be serious. I kept taking aspirins."

"Your uncle said you're visiting from the United States. Did you have any immunization before you came?"

"Just smallpox."

"I think the best thing to do is to take you to the hospital right now and give you some tests. I'll drive you over."

"You're taking her to the hospital?" my mother asked.

"She's had this pain for a while now." He thought for a moment. "It could be any number of things—a virus, or from her heart—although that's only a remote possibility."

"I'll come with you," my mother said.

"No, no, that's not a good idea at this hour. You can come and see her tomorrow. Don't worry, we'll take care of her," Dr. Majid said, and turned to me. "I'll wait outside for you. Take what you need for two, three days. We may have to give you a number of tests."

"That long?" my mother protested. "She just got here and you're taking her to the hospital."

He smiled and then said, "I'm doing what I can."

In the car I lay my head back and looked at the streets through half-closed eyes. The electricity was turned off after a certain hour and moonlight shone over men or families sleeping on sidewalks or cats sniffing at garbage. Insects screeched.

I must send a telegram to Tony immediately, I thought. But the thought gave me little consolation.

I sat up and tried to distract myself by talking to Dr. Majid. "How long have you been practicing here? My mother said you went to school in the United States."

"I've been here for six years now. But you're only visiting, aren't you?"

"Yes," I said. "I hadn't seen my mother since I was a child. I came to visit my father, then found out about her."

He turned and looked at me with curiosity. I gave him a brief account of my mother's disappearance when I was a child. He listened intently. His curiosity and attentiveness

made me like him and be less afraid of going to the hospital.
It had been nice of him to come to see me in the middle
of the night and then drive me over.

"Where in the United States do you live?" he asked.

"In Lexington right now, but we're thinking of moving
back to Cambridge or Boston."

"Lexington is a real suburb, isn't it?"

"Yes," I said. "Where did you live?"

"Mostly in Ann Arbor. That's where I got my degree.
Then I practiced a while in New York and Boston actually."

"Lucky to find someone like you here. To tell you the
truth I was afraid of what kind of a doctor I'd get."

"I don't blame you."

"Do you live here with your family?"

"I'm not married."

"I meant with your parents." I found myself blushing.

"No, I have a little house a few streets from the hospital.
There's a garden around it. A gardener comes in once a week
and makes sure there are flowers all year."

"It sounds lovely."

"I like it."

"Don't you find Kashan a little depressing?"

"Depressing? Not at all. When you're better, take a walk
around and see how much variety there is to the architec-
ture, for instance. Those houses left from hundreds of years
ago, along with the shabbiest huts, and then there are these
modern houses."

I was silent, acutely homesick again for the almost uniform houses in Lexington with their open green lawns and
white shingles. The liveliness I had felt while talking to the
doctor began to waver.

He listened to my silence and said, "Maybe you don't

see my point. Everything might seem haphazard and artless to you."

"I can see getting used to it," I said. Then unable to help myself, I said, "But what do you do in your free time? There is nothing to do here."

"I have close friends here and that's important. There are a lot of places to take excursions to on the weekends, and in the evenings you can always find a good restaurant and an occasional good movie."

We passed a rivulet, not much wider than the gutters running along every street. Two young boys were swimming there, splashing water around and at each other. The moon flooded their bodies. Dr. Majid looked at them wistfully.

"Look, doesn't that seem like fun to you?"

"What made you choose Kashan?" I asked.

"I knew I wanted to practice in Iran. When I came back I visited a lot of places and I liked Kashan the best. It's so peaceful here."

"But maybe not very exciting," I persisted.

"Depends on what you mean by exciting."

We had reached the hospital—an old grayish building. I almost choked with anxiety at the sight of it.

Dr. Majid drove into the parking lot and, perhaps sensing my fear, he said, "The hospital isn't as bad as it looks. We just got some new equipment and we have some very good doctors and nurses."

"You'll be seeing me, right? Not another doctor?"

"Yes, don't worry about it."

He got out of the car and I followed.

Inside, he disappeared into a dim, long corridor. I gave the woman behind the reception desk the necessary information and waited. The walls were full of stains—of medicine, blood?—and flies settled on them freely. Three women, wearing black *chadors*, huddled together on a bench across from me, occasionally swaying together as though they were glued to one another.

Two men came in, carrying a stretcher with a body wrapped up in a sheet and everyone perked up, looking at them. The men stood there, motionless, still holding the stretcher while the woman behind the desk rang a bell. A nurse came and led them in.

"Heart attack," one of the women said.

"There was blood on the sheet," said the one sitting next to her.

"I heard some people have died of typhoid in Khasvin," the third woman said.

"We have only one life; we all die one way or the other."

"Once God wills our end there's nothing we can do about it."

"Only my sins make me afraid of dying."

"You're worried about your sins—you with your angelic ways."

A nurse came out of the corridor and approached me.

"You must be Feri McIntosh," she said.

I nodded.

"I'm sorry I took so long but I was with another patient. She doesn't want to be in the hospital and was causing a lot of trouble."

I got up and followed her through the corridor to a room. She was young with small black eyes and heavy eyebrows. She had replaced the buttons on her white uniform with heart-shaped lacquered ones. She gave me a white robe and pointed to a dressing space for me to change. I stepped behind the curtain, thinking it was comforting that the white robe looked like any other hospital robe.

The nurse was very lively and talked all the time as she gave me the routine tests—weighing me, taking my blood pressure, taking blood from my arm. She said her name was Manijeh.

"I hear you're visiting from the United States," she said. "I'd like to visit there one day. My fiance is an engineer. When we are married we may go, but first we'll have to save some money. You know Doctor Majid studied there?"

"Yes."

"He says going there will only make us restless and dissatisfied."

"Maybe he has a point."

"They accept nothing, the Americans; they think they can change the world so they can be happy. Life goes on— you can't change a thing. Dr. Majid is temperamental. Maybe he's caught some of that restlessness himself."

Manijeh led me to another room, where she gave me X-rays and then we came back to the first room to wait for Dr. Majid.

"You're in good hands," she said, leaning against the wall. "Since he came here he has done so much for the hospital. We have new equipment, journals to read."

She sat down as if she had nothing else to do but talk to me. "What do you think of houses in the U.S.—they have no walls around them. Don't you lose your privacy?"

"Actually Americans are always worried about their privacy."

There was a shrill cry in the corridor, followed by "No, no, please." We turned towards the door and listened.

"It must be the old woman who was being admitted before you," Manijeh said. "She has cancer and has to be operated on but she's very religious and doesn't want to be seen by male doctors—all our surgeons are men."

The sound of crying became louder and then I could see an old woman, wearing the hospital robe and a kerchief, dragged along by a nurse and a young woman.

"Let me die in peace, please let me die," the old woman pleaded.

Dr. Majid came in, wearing a white uniform. He asked me to sit on the cot in the corner and began to give me more tests—looking into my eyes, ears, pulling my shoulders backward, examining my breasts. Manijeh stood there watching him, with an expression of humility and absolute respect. Then he left and came back quickly. "Nothing shows in the X-rays. And we can't give you further tests until we have the results of the blood test."

"When is that going to be?"

"In a couple of days," he said.

Then Manijeh took me to the room, where I was to stay, a large room, with a wrought iron bed, shiny olive-green walls, and matching green curtains. In a corner stood a refrigerator, a table, and two chairs. The air felt hot and stifling. She turned on a ceiling fan and looked around as if to inspect the room.

"We have only four rooms for private care—they used to be for doctors to sleep in—that's why there's a refrigerator here." She rubbed her finger on the table and held it before me. "Look at the dust. You'd think no one had stayed here for years. Well, probably no one has."

"Where do most patients stay?"

"In the ward. That's what most of them can afford. We have these rooms, a small ward, and a large clinic."

I realized that I had not even asked the price of the

room. "How much is it a night here?"

"About $30, I think."

I nodded. At least the cost was not staggering.

"Go to bed now. I'll be back with some medicine for you in a minute."

I looked at the sheets, almost expecting to find a bug there as I had in the hotel room, but the sheets were clean with that soft blue color from bleach.

I got into my own nightgown and lay in bed. I tried to think of Tony, of my experiments in the laboratory, but the past was hard to grasp. I tried to think of the future but it seemed devoid of meaning. Only my illness—the pain, the uncertainty, and the idea of being in that remote and rather primitive hospital—had a hold on me.

Manijeh came back with the medicine and water. The medicine was a white powder on a folded piece of wax paper.

"What's that?" I asked, looking at it suspiciously. It reminded me of a medicine I once took as a child.

"It's just a pain killer," she said. "Like aspirin—only this is much stronger."

Reluctantly I put the powder in the back of my mouth and drank a full glass of water. A bitter taste trickled down my throat for a long time.

Manijeh turned off the light before leaving. I tried to sleep but a fly caught in the dark buzzed frantically, keeping me awake. Then two cats began to fight somewhere, making angry, shrill cries. Finally I could hear intermittent moans. I assumed it was the woman I had seen dragged along the corridor, and I kept imagining her as a translucent body with dark lines of cancer branched out through it. Then I thought of my own body that way with the painful spots shining in dark blood, red or dismembered and scattered on different tables with students poring over the pieces, the way I had practiced on dead animals when I had been a student. The slightly putrid smell, the cold slimy touch. At first that part of biology had almost turned me against the subject but gradually I had gotten used to it. Now I could dissect a frog, a rabbit, a mouse—my hands steady.

10

Rows and rows of rats crawled on the ground and began to climb the walls, onto the ceiling. The room was large and echoless. Bright lights glared on the rats and the tubes lining the shelves on one wall, tubes full of yellow chemicals. The rats all gathered on the ceiling, covering every inch. Then they began to fall one by one, on my head, shoulders, hands. I screamed but no sound came out of my throat.

Someone shook me.

"I think you were having a bad dream," Manijeh said.

I sighed with relief. "I did have an awful dream about rats crawling around."

The dream was not all that unrealistic. I had once used fifty rats in an experiment on the effect of thorazine on their eating behavior—would the ones on the tranquilizer eat less or more, faster or slower. Late one evening I had come in to check on them and discovered that the cages were open —carelessness on my assistant's part, probably—and rats crawled on the floor. I had stifled a scream. Later I almost fired my assistant. She had begun to make other similar blunders. She underfed some mice, for instance, and I found them on the verge of starvation.

I started to worry about my work which I had managed

to push out of my mind for a while. So many things could go wrong with the experiments I had left in her care. Chemicals congealing in tubes, she not properly recording the data. I resolved to write to her immediately and also send a telegram to Tony. He would get it as soon as he returned from his trip.

I asked Manijeh how to go about sending the telegram. She said I should write down the message and she would phone it for me.

She pulled open the curtains and soft sunlight flowed in. Behind the window there was a fig tree, and sparrows hopped on its branches.

"How's the pain?" she asked, wrapping the cloth around my arm to take my blood pressure.

"It's still there. The medicine doesn't seem to help." I had awakened a couple of times during the night with acute pain.

She took my pulse, gave me a pad and a pen, and then left the room.

I sat up in bed. I could see the garden with its small flowered paths in the back of the hospital. An old woman, wearing the hospital robe, sat on a bench while a young girl fed her. Men, women, and children, the relatives of patients, wandered around or sat on benches, talking.

I jotted down on a piece of paper a few words about the letter of permission I needed and the illness. I also wrote a brief letter to my assistant, telling her of my situation and urging her to supervise the experiments closely.

Manijeh came back with breakfast on a tray. She rolled up my bed and put the tray before me.

I gave her the telegram to Tony and asked her if I could

have an envelope and stamp for the letter to my assistant. She said she would bring them to me.

I ate some of the food—eggs, bread, and a glass of hot milk—with little appetite.

Dr. Majid came in, followed by Manijeh.

"I hear you're still in pain," he said, standing by my bed.

"Maybe I should go back to Teheran—there must be better hospitals there." I was complaining and bad-tempered, I knew, but could not help it.

"At this point, this hospital is as good as any for you. We're just giving you preliminary tests. Travelling could only do you harm."

His eyes, half-hidden under puffy lids, reflected personal affront.

"It's the uncertainty. At least if I knew what it is. I wish I had never taken this trip."

"We'll know what's wrong in a couple of days. The minute we have the results of the blood tests, we'll know where to go from there." He held my wrist and began to count my pulse.

"Everything is normal—her temperature, blood pressure," Manijeh said.

He let go of my hand. "I'll put you on a stronger medicine for now," he said and they both left.

My mother and uncle came in near noon—there seemed to be few visiting restrictions in the hospital and the garden was always filled with visitors. My mother was panting a little from the walk. They brought flowers and food for the nurse to heat up and serve to me for lunch.

The room became filled with the aroma of the flowers—jasmin, lilacs, and roses. On the ceramic vase holding the flowers there was a picture of a man and a woman sitting under a willow tree drinking wine.

My mother and uncle sat on chairs beside me and for a little while we were silent.

"You'll get better," my mother said at last. "I've been praying for you."

"Yes, you'll get better," my uncle said.

"I hope you're right," I said.

My uncle looked at me directly. "Remember me when I used to be able to see?" he asked suddenly.

"Yes," I said. The recollection was vague.

"You would never get tired of making me chase you around or carry you on my shoulders."

"Have you shown your eyes to any good doctors?"

"To every doctor in so many cities. I spent most of my savings on it—remember I used to fix old bicycles and sell them—but it was no use. I worried about my eyes constantly. I was sad and withdrawn for months. Then, one day, a revelation came to me. I was finding my way across the street with my cane. A car made a harsh, screeching sound and a man started shouting obscenities at me. 'Why don't you watch out, you son of a bitch. I almost ran you over.' I stood there, my whole body shaking. I left the street and found a tree to sit under. I kept shaking for a long time. Then I had a strong vision. I saw layer and layer of flesh being removed from me like cotton until my skeleton was revealed. The skeleton began to walk, making clanking sounds, and then it too began to come apart, collapsing into powder. Yet, as I watched my body disintegrating, I felt something in me coming alive, something that made me see that tree with its green leaves, a woman with a red skirt gathering something from the field across the road. I felt the tree, the scenery around me. . . ."

My mother had closed her eyes and was praying. She pursed her lips and blew her breath into my face as if forcing the prayer on me physically.

She opened her eyes.

"Remember you were sick once and kept saying, 'shake me, shake me!'" She moved her head rhythmically and laughed. "You said, 'shake me like a rug.'"

"You must have had fever," my uncle said.

"A neighbor had just died—Hamideh *khanom*—you were very attached to her. You kept saying, 'pick her up and hang her on the wall.'" She laughed again.

"I remember her," I said. "She was a tall, sturdy looking woman."

"You used to get so attached to everyone we knew and they to you. You'd go from house to house, visiting. I had to look for you all over every day."

"Yes," I said.

"One day, after I had left, I asked a neighbor to go and see you for me. She said you'd become very withdrawn and wouldn't talk to anyone. You'd changed." She began to stare at her hands.

We were all silent again. I closed my eyes and thought about that childhood illness.

I had been feverish all day and I woke up in the middle of the night to shadows all around. I sat up to see my mother, father, and a group of men and women sitting on two separate rugs. Oil lamps hung on a tree and on the arch of the hallway. . . . I stayed in bed for what seemed like weeks. I would trace the intricate designs on the rug below my bed or look at the pattern on the ceiling. Sometimes my mother would sit in the corner of the room, cross-legged, fanning herself, reading the Koran, or cleaning out grains of rice and beans. She would give me a bowl of multicolored beans to play with—red, yellow, black, white with a black heart—and I would separate them and line them up like marbles. Once she gave me a crystal drop from a chandelier and I held it against the sun, excited by the richness of the color it produced. Finally a new doctor came and gave my mother some capsules for me. I was well in a few days. "That doctor did a miracle," my mother had said. "It was God's will to send him to us."

I was given more and more medication but the pain persisted.

Hours, several days passed. I had not heard from Tony. I asked Manijeh if there was a way to call the United States from the hospital. "That wouldn't be easy," she said. "The connection with other countries is very bad here. Sometimes it can take hours to get through and even then the voices won't be very clear. Some of our doctors have tried and given up."

I decided to wait. Tony might have extended his trip or perhaps my telegram was still on the way, slow in delivery. . . . My emotions became dull and colorless as if they had been bleached.

My mother and uncle came in frequently and brought me books, a radio, more flowers, and food. My mother would massage my back, pray for me, and read *surehs* from the Koran. A few times she insisted on staying there with me overnight but that was one rule the hospital tried to observe rigidly, otherwise the place would be filled with relatives.

I tried to read the books they brought. The effort to ease myself back into reading Persian would take my mind off the pain for a while. Mahmood Majid loaned me a couple of novels by a well-known Persian author. It was so long since I had had time to read novels. It was nice to be able to do so now. The attitude towards women, or the excessiveness of male-female love expressed in the books made me laugh out loud. But my pleasure soon would turn to despair and I would fling the book on the table and try to sleep, forget.

At times the thought of my experiments filled me with a different kind of anxiety—how pointless and frivolous it all was. What did protein in the brains of rats have to do with people's problems and concerns? Those endless hours of research and the money spent seemed to be no more than an expensive game to keep me and others like me amused.

On the eighth day Dr. Majid came in early in the morning. His uniform was creased and his hair disheveled as if he had just gotten out of bed.

"We know what's wrong with you" he said immediately, looking flushed.

I barely glanced at him. I was in a state near stupor. "What?"

"Nothing like what we expected—you've been completely on the wrong kind of medication."

"What, what's wrong with me?" I was suddenly aroused.

"You have an ulcer."

"An ulcer! No, it can't be. After all this—I don't believe it." Instead of relief that the illness had turned out to be something less than fatal I felt oddly disappointed.

"There's no question about it. It shows clearly on the

X-ray we took of your stomach. Sometimes the pain is projected to another part of the body. It's just something that we didn't expect at all and didn't look for. And of course all that aspirin we were giving you only aggravated it."

"All the tension of the trip must have done it," I said defensively.

He shook his head. "It's a very big ulcer. You must have had it for a long time—a year or two. Only the pain has been dormant."

"I've had it that long?"

"You brought it with you." He smiled. "Now you have no right to be afraid of the hospital, me, or your country. What you have is a Western disease."

He emphasized the word, *Western.*

I was quiet. Suddenly there seemed to be no air in the room. I was thirty-two years old and had an ulcer.

11

"Maybe you weren't very happy, or else why come back after all these years!" My father's words had particular significance now as I lay in that remote hospital with an ulcer.

I took out a mirror from my pocketbook and looked at my face, studying it for signs of unhappiness. My hair had become stringy, my cheeks hollow, and I had dark circles under my eyes. A haunted look, what might be expected from a person who had lain in bed for so long in fear and uncertainty. But beneath those signs I saw scars. Scars of pain brushed aside. Dissatisfactions not coped with. Memories rolled before me like a rug, worn and faded in some spots and vivid in others.

I am pregnant and we have just moved to a house in Lexington. Boxes in different stages of unpacking lie around the living room. From one window I can see birds circling in the air, smoke swirling out of the chimneys of the houses across the street. Children play on swings and in the sandbox in a playground, and their mothers sit together, talking or reading.

In a way I am envious of women who are home and taking care of their children, but I cannot bear the thought of taking time off from work. There is always work to do—papers at different stages of revision, experiments, appointments, colloquia, conventions, and a book for which I have signed a contract that is supposed to be finished within the year. Then there is the course I am taking a couple of evenings a week—Japanese brush painting—which is meant to be relief from work.

Tony is upstairs, looking at the first edition of Darwin's *Origin of Species* he has just purchased.

I call to him to come down and help me unpack.

"I'll be down in a minute," he says. "I'm just checking something."

He spends hours sometimes checking and cataloguing these books.

"This is really not the time for it," I say.

"Just wait one minute. I'll be down."

Moments pass. I hear him swear to himself a couple of times.

I open the boxes and put dishes in the kitchen cabinets, records and books onto shelves.

Tony comes down the circular stairway, holding the book.

"A page is missing," he says. "I'll have to go to the bookstore before it closes."

He dashes out of the door before I have a chance to say anything.

Opening a box, I cut my thumb. I go to the sink, wash the cut and bandage it. I am on the verge of crying. This would only slow things down. Last time we moved, we had boxes sitting around for weeks, for months. This time it is important to get things out of the way before the baby comes. And all that shopping we must do for the baby. I wonder if Tony is going to cooperate or disappear all the time at crucial moments.

The phone rings. It is my assistant. Something has gone wrong with one of the experiments. I am needed immediately. I go over and stay until midnight.

When I come back Tony is asleep and the boxes are exactly as I had left them. I go to bed but cannot sleep for a long time, thinking of Tony's selfishness, of the experiment which has gone wrong, the baby. What if it is born with a deformity, what if it is the kind of child who cries all night or is sick constantly?

I get up in the morning, tired, with a nausea that stays with me all day. . . .

It is another day. A young, dark-haired woman knocks at my door. She introduces herself as Jane, and tells me that she lives in the house next to ours.

"I came to welcome you and also to invite you to a party on Saturday night."

"Thank you, we'd love to come. I just have to check with my husband." Between Tony and me the calendar is always full of appointments. "Is it all right if I let you know tomorrow?"

"Of course. You'll meet some of the people in the neighborhood." She looks toward her house expectantly. "I'd better dash now. I hope you can make it to the party."

Their house, on the night of the party, is dark and smoky.

People have clustered in small groups and some are dancing in the center to loud music. The air smells of marijuana and food. I had been feeling nauseous all day and almost did not come. But showing up at social occasions is as important an obligation as work.

Jane comes over and introduces herself to Tony and then takes us around to meet her husband and the other guests. She is wearing a black dress with huge green poppies on it, which make her pale green eyes seem larger. She is prettier than I had thought at first. Her husband Rob is thin, tall, dark, and laconic, his voice heavy with boredom. In a way they are perfectly matched physically with their almost identical coloring, slow deliberate manner, and the insistent way they look into people's eyes when they speak.

A little girl wearing a grown-up's slip, rouge, and lipstick stands above the staircase, looking down.

"Is that your little girl?" Tony asks. "She looks like Jean Harlow."

"She's my wife's child from her first marriage. But we hope she's not going to be spoiled by all the comments about her looks. We would like her to grow up to be a serious person," Rob says.

"It would be nice if you could control such things," I say.

A tall, red-headed woman standing beside us, says, "I feel people with better genes should produce as many children as possible."

Another woman, standing a step away, glances at her husband. "He may get the Nobel Prize. I have to keep the children out of the way, the house has to be constantly quiet."

"I know, it's hard to live with a brilliant man. What makes things even harder for me is that we're in the same field."

They say all this in utter seriousness. But I cannot help thinking: everyone works hard while I get stuck with morning sickness. I must work longer hours in the evening.

A very tall, balding man comes over and puts his arm around the red-headed woman. "Honey," she says to him, "I was just telling them how hard it is for me to keep up with you."

"Yes," he says, not smiling.

Jane and Tony walk away to dance. The two women and the man are absorbed in talking to each other.

"So you're a biologist," Rob says to me. "I'm studying law but I'm really more interested in motorcycles. Would you care to dance?"

I shake my head. "I really don't feel well. I almost didn't come tonight." I feel a surge of nausea again, now mixed with slight cramps.

"Maybe you need fresh air, it's getting stuffy here. Would you like to go for a ride on my motorcycle?"

"No thanks," I try to smile. The smile seems to dissolve, spread over my face, drip into the room. The room becomes dark-gray and distant, the voices fuzzy. I realize I am exceedingly high on marijuana and wine. "I think I'd better go home now."

"Are you sure, so soon?"

"We'll get together again."

I wave to Tony, dancing, and go back home. I lie on the bed with my clothes on, wondering if something is seriously wrong. I stare into darkness, at the flickers of light that pass by the window. There seems to be a momentary relief but then I realize that I had fallen asleep. The nausea and cramps are worse.

The luminous dial on my watch reads 3:30 and Tony is

still not back. He said he wanted to go to bed early so that he could get some work done in the morning. I have flashes of him leaning too closely over various women, touches, a kiss, and close my eyes as if that would exorcise jealousy. "You're just insecure," he would say if confronted with it. Or, "Grow up," or "You know I don't have time for these things."

I hear his footsteps approaching. I pretend to be asleep.

I begin to have more cramps, on and off. I consult my gynecologist and he says you must rest in bed for a while. I spend a day in bed listening to the radio, reading the *Boston Globe*, going over a research paper I am writing on hormones in the brain that I think *Science* might publish. I have a yearning to talk to someone, a female friend, about the pregnancy and motherhood, to just talk. In my head I go over the list of people Tony and I know. I have developed no intimate friendships for the last few years. I make a resolution to try to make friends, knowing full well I probably will not want to spare the time.

I go back to work the next day. I am a little pale and distraught but that might be from having stayed in bed for a whole day. My rats greet me with their tiny red eyes from their cages. Then I go to my office and shut the door. In a few hours I have cramps again, more persistently now. A sudden dizziness comes over me. The world becomes blank. I literally feel something going out of me. I crumble on the chair. Then with more courage I examine myself. Blood seeps out of me, spot by spot. I ring Tony. Luckily he's at his desk. "I'll call an ambulance for you right now," he says urgently.

I wrap the white laboratory coat around me and wait.

In the hospital I have a miscarriage. The inception of a fetus embodied in thick blood. It was hardly alive, no more than a conglomerate of cells. Tony arrives immediately afterwards.

"You should have stayed in bed for a few days," my gynecologist says, gently admonishing. "As I advised you."

"I told her the same thing," Tony remarks. He had never told me that.

I can see as he stands there, hunched over with his eyes latching on to various objects to avoid eye contact, that he does not feel comfortable in the role of a father, or the father of a lost child. Tony, at ease in every social situation, as husband, lover, son, is not comfortable in the new role in which he was about to be cast. Sympathy for him fills me and I reach out and squeeze his hand. The sympathy is lost a few hours later as he begins to lecture me. "Maybe deep down you didn't want the baby," or "You could go and see a psychiatrist."

Because I was at the early stages of pregnancy the miscarriage does not have a major physical impact on me. In fact, the doctor says I can attempt to get pregnant any time I want. The consensus Tony and I reach is to wait for a while. The names, Susan, Cyrus, Ivan, Sarah, have to be discarded for the time being. The baby clothes, the furniture, must be put away. Everything—the bed, the house, even the laboratory—is a little colder without the fetus growing in me, with the knowledge that it is lost.

I work even harder, keeping up a frantic pace until I collapse and sleep for fifteen or twenty hours to compensate. We rarely entertain or go to the movies we used to enjoy so much. We seldom spend leisurely evenings together. At work I am erratic, blood rising and falling in my face at the slightest provocation.

There is a certain sterility about the long, quiet halls of the laboratory with only the automatic equipment tap-tapping. It is as if people walk on tiptoe or have their hands on their mouths when they speak. The atmosphere no longer seems particularly congenial. Conversations in the luncheonette across the street or occasionally in our offices stay close to shoptalk, rarely touching on the personal. My assistant, whose enthusiasm about work had been encouraging, appears scatterbrained and superficial in her ideas. My boss, whose attention to detail I had always admired, seems overly fastidious. I could look for a job somewhere else, consider teaching rather than only doing research. . . .

This is just a state of mind. I am tired.

In an attempt to slow down a bit I take long walks in the neighborhood. Once on the street behind our house, I see Tony in Jane's house. He is leaning over the kitchen counter with a drink in his hand and talking to Jane. She is leaning also, looking at Tony and smiling. I pause for an instant and then walk away quickly.

On another day, as I am walking through a street, a motorcycle roars and comes to a stop beside me.

"Taking a walk?" It is Rob's voice. He is wearing a leather jacket and a crash helmet.

"Just wandering around."

"I was thinking of taking a ride through the country." He looks me in the eyes—an inviting stare.

I try to assess my feelings. What do I have to lose?

"I've never ridden a motorcycle. It might be fun."

I get on, wrapping my arms around his waist. Gravel

pops from under the wheels and I think of bubbles bursting. The wind blows through my blouse and hair and I feel like laughing.

In a secluded, wooded area outside of Concord, he stops his motorcycle. We sit side by side on a grassy spot and he takes out a marijuana cigarette, already rolled. We smoke until the birds begin to sound more melodic; the sun seems softer, teasing our skins, the sky mellower and more blue. My arm, where he has held it, is pulsing. I watch his eyes going over me. He pulls me to himself and we kiss, a long easy kiss.

He lies on the grass and I lie down also, putting my head on his arm.

An hour or so later, going back, he says, "I think I know a little about your body now, how to turn it on. It will be easier next time."

Next time. The thought of a continuity with him destroys my lightheartedness.

"You're so quiet," he says.

The reality around me begins to blur; Tony, Rob and Jane, my co-workers, becoming clumsy sketches of themselves, faded, without substance. Tony and I stop talking, talk in a real sense. I wake in the middle of the night sometimes and just sit and stare into the dark. . . .

"You should see a psychiatrist," Tony says.

I shrug. "I don't want to."

12

Manijeh had said I could leave any time. I got into my regular clothes and began to pack.

There was a knock at the door and Dr. Majid came in.

"So you're leaving," he said, sitting down on one of the chairs. "May I ask you something—what is it that troubles you? An ulcer is a bodily signal of the distress of the soul." He spoke seriously in the manner of a priest.

"Nothing specific, everything," I said, sitting on a chair also. "I just had not faced up to things. I had let things go and pile up."

"Is your husband an American?"

"Yes," I said.

"I thought so," he said. "That automatically compels you to go back to the United States."

"Him and my work," I said, without conviction. I was no longer sure what I was going back for.

"I guessed you'd have some kind of a career. What do you do?"

"I'm a biologist. Strictly research work. I used to think I'd hate teaching—public speaking. I'm not sure of that now."

"Biology." He seemed a little surprised. "I had pictured

you in something else—in history or literature."

"We all have our stereotypes. I wouldn't have guessed you were a doctor."

"What then?"

"I'd put you more in academia or in the arts. A violinist, maybe."

"A violinist?" He laughed, then got up. "I assume you haven't seen much of Kashan. Let me take you to some places while you're still here."

"That would be very nice."

"I'll come over one afternoon this week." He started for the door. Then he turned around and said, "Take the antacid medicine as I said, go easy on spices, and most importantly, try to relax."

I left the hospital, one thought swirling in my head: that I must change things, drastically. I decided to walk to my mother's house, to get rid of some of the agitated energy inside of me.

Near the hospital there was a busy street, and just beyond it stretched vast, uninhabited spaces. Small mud houses stood next to grand ones with pretty urns of flowers set on their doorsteps. Donkeys, camels, and cars travelled side by side.

I wondered if I could learn to like a place such as this and even prefer it to American cities, as Mahmood Majid did. Thinking of Mahmood Majid filled me with a sense of security as if I was wrapped in a wool blanket in the middle of a cold winter. I wondered if he had women friends he felt very close to.

I came to a food market with carts full of fruit and vegetables, and shops stacked with cheeses and spices. Women holding live chickens sat against walls, next to laborers, beggars, and idle men passing rosaries between their fingers. The chickens, bound by their feet, flapped occasionally, feathers coming off them and floating in the air which smelled heavily of spices. I sniffed in the aroma and thought: for a long time I will not be able to indulge in spicy food the way I did before, go to the kind of restaurants I was so fond of.

A little dark-haired, red-cheeked girl walked beside her mother, looking at different carts and windows. I stood for a moment and watched her, her gestures. I watched the faces of other people. Suspended between those faces and scenes were the first eighteen years of my life. I had tried to make them into shadows; they had reappeared as nightmares.

Then I went from cart to cart, touching the fruit, asking the prices. The nasal voices of vendors advertising their merchandise, the hum of shoppers mingling with the sounds of metals from the blacksmiths in the bazaar surrounded me. I bought fresh figs, pomegranates, and white grapes, the fruits my mother liked. The shopkeeper, small as a child, with a dry dark skin, picked them carefully, one by one, and weighed them in separate bags on a brass scale hanging on the door.

My mother and uncle were waiting for me. It was as if they had had nothing to do for years and now had finally found something. On her way home, at lunch, Manijeh had stopped by their house to tell them I would be home and about the ulcer.

I followed my mother to the other side of the courtyard where she said she had furnished a room for me. There was a bed, a cane chair in the corner of the room, and several earthen vases full of flowers. A bluish rug and bluish curtains gave the room the aura of a tile bath.

"You went through all this trouble for me. I don't even know how much longer I'll be here," I said. "I want to buy a house for you, something more comfortable than this."

She looked surprised. "At my age moving is no good. Besides I'm used to this house—I've lived in it for so long. I know all the neighbors around me."

"Fine, if that's how you really feel."

"I want you to be as comfortable as possible here. You must relax—what you've got shows you've suffered." She looked at the sky as if pleading with God. "What I did to you couldn't be easily undone."

"You mustn't feel that way," I said.

Her face trembled a little as if in a spasm and then she merely sighed and left the room.

I spent the rest of the day reading, listening to a radio my uncle brought over, or looking out of the window at the dark, bent heads of children playing. Moths floated into the room like bits of paper.

My uncle sat for long hours in a shady corner in the courtyard smoking his water pipe, smiling, dozing off, dreaming. My mother worked slowly, shopping, cooking, watering the plants. She did not let me help, saying, "You must rest for a while now."

Neighbors came in—a very thin tall woman, a young girl with fat red cheeks who laughed a lot, an older woman leaning on a cane. (Of the thin woman, my uncle said later, that her husband's first wife had put a spell on her; of the young girl, I don't understand how she can smile like that, her husband beats her every night; of the old woman—that she was a hundred and one years old.)

They talked, mostly about a funeral, a wedding, how the water had run dry in some gutters, premonition of someone's death, dreams about the possibility of an earthquake. They sighed loudly from time to time and said they would have to wait for God's will and there was no point in trying to change things. They always spoke in low melancholy tones which seemed to be more from habit than anything else.

Then night fell with its usual suddenness. Again, the voice of the muezzin, other sounds mixing to make a muffled but incessant moan, and a little later, the incredible display of the stars.

My mother took me to a room in the adjacent courtyard. She carried a naphtha lamp with her and set it down on a mantel in the room. Except for a battered trunk covered with velveteen, and a few other items—oversized pots, pans, and trays—the room was empty. She opened the trunk and took out different items.

"These were yours when you were a little girl. I kept them with me and looked at them and rubbed them against my face when I got too lonely." She held some children's clothing before me—a red-checkered dress, one in baby-blue. "For a moment it would seem you were with me."

"I remember I took a rag doll you'd bought for me to bed every night," I said.

"This is a picture of you just before I left," she said, taking out an enlarged and faded photograph from the bottom of the trunk.

I looked at it for a long time.

In the photograph I was sitting on a wooden chair with a high back, holding a rose in my hand. It suddenly seemed time had congealed with me caught in it.

"Did you ever regret leaving my father?" I asked. I had avoided the subject so far.

She paused for a long time and I was sorry I had asked.

"At the time I had no choice. It was as though someone had opened the door of a prison for me and I had to run out."

"Wasn't it like being in prison later, too? Is this life what you expected?"

"At least now I have only myself to blame."

Then, in a voice not so much wistful as incredulous, she told me how she would first steal only glimpses of that man as he came to work, and how one day a single look between them sealed them together. She described the subsequent brief meetings between them, the guilt, the fear, the fits of depression and crying following every meeting, how they both finally decided to avoid seeing each other for a while and how those days were even more hellish than the time when they did see each other.

Then one night she was awakened by the sound of gravel being thrown against the window. She tiptoed to the window and looked out. In the moonlight she could see him, the man, signalling to her to come down. She would not have gone except for the expression on his face. He looked so wan and drawn out. He was unshaven and his hair disheveled. She put her *chador* on, but before going down, she came into my room and looked at me. Then she went to the outside door and opened it. Standing in the privacy of the doorway, she and the man talked for a long time, whispering. Their voices were quieter than the ripples of water running in the gutters. He told her that he had locked himself in a room and had not eaten for days. That he seemed to be living in hell already and so he might as well sin and persuade another man's wife to go away with him. That night they agreed to leave together for a village not far from Teheran. Once safely settled with him there, she would come back and take me away. She planned to talk my father into giving her a divorce.

The next night she left with the man in a horsecart he brought to the wider street a block away. As they rode away in the horsecart she hid her face in her *chador* and cried. For days all she did was cry.

My mother stopped talking suddenly and began to put back the things she had taken out of the trunk.

"Why do you suppose he changed so much later?" I asked.

"I don't know. He was such a nice man. Maybe our sin finally poisoned him."

I realized she had never referred to him by his name. I asked her that.

"Sohrab," she said. "But after a while I stopped calling him anything."

By the door, just before leaving, she put her hands around my head and kissed me.

"Do you forgive me?" she asked.

"Of course, of course."

"How could you?" she said softly, rhetorically.

The next day I stood in the doorway of my room and watched her. She dawdled instead of walking. Her arms and hands looked swollen and her skin was sallow, but her expression seemed livelier than in that first encounter when I arrived in Kashan.

She turned and looked at me.

"Feri," she called. "You want to come out?"

Her voice was so real, so familiar. I went out into the courtyard. I sat at the edge of the pool, shaded by a wide eucalyptus tree, with one of my hands dangling in the water, and we talked some more.

It was one of those lukewarm breezy mornings that makes one expectant that things will happen. As I listened, her voice became monotonous and blurred, even more ghost-like than it had been the night before.

My father had not given her much trouble once she had left. He must have felt too disgraced. He gave her a divorce readily. They did not even encounter each other in court. He was willing to divorce her without requiring her presence and he did it within the first few days after she left. I was the only thing he held from her. Every time she asked for me he refused, and he made it legally impossible for her to get near me. She could not really blame him after what she had done to him.

She and the man got married immediately in a little mosque off a shrine. Then they spent the day in the holy place. Neither one of them was eager to leave as though the longer they stayed at the shrine the more sanctified their marriage, the more purified.

At first it was easy to live just for him. The village was primitive with one short main street and a few dirt roads. They lived in a tiny house with two rooms.

She spent the day at household chores while he went to work in Teheran, doing accounting for different families. In the evening before he came, she would sweep an area in the yard and spread a mattress for them to sleep on and would have the dinner all ready to serve. He told her of the events of the day as they ate. They huddled together in bed, awake for hours. Not from fear—although it would have been justifiable in that isolated place—but from a kind of almost unnatural exhilaration. They shuddered in each others' arms. He was an inarticulate man and his emotions exploded sometimes, making him rough with her. On the days he did not work they took excursions on donkeys to other villages or to a shrine.

One evening he was late coming home. She went back and forth between the two windows in the room and looked for him. He came home late and ate his supper very quickly. When she asked him why he was so late, he said his work took that long, but she knew something was bothering him. That night she had a dream, which began to recur, about passing through a succession of alleys and ending up before a dark, deep stairway. The steps were wet and slippery and very steep. She had to descend without knowing why. The fear woke her.

After that the man was his old self for a while and then was late again one evening. She heard knocks at the door. Hesitantly she went to open it. A group of beggars stood there asking for food. They were an awful-looking bunch, mutilated in an arm or a leg. She went inside to get some food and they followed her and sat down on the rug in the courtyard. She was not sure what they wanted. For a long time they refused to leave. They just sat there, not even talking, mute and frightening. After they left she waited for him by the window again. There was no electricity then, and she first saw him coming by the glow of his cigar. She ran out to him and clutched at his arm, begging him never to leave her alone for so long. Inside she hinted that she had given up a lot for him and that threw him into a fit—he began to smash everything—dishes, a vase, a mirror.

A few days later they left the village and she stayed with relatives in Teheran while he went to Kashan to set up a house for them. That was when she hid in the basement, too ashamed to be seen by anyone, when she tried to drown herself in the cistern. Sometimes she took long, aimless walks which would always end at our house. She stood in a hallway nearby and watched for me. Once she saw me wearing an ugly loose-fitting dress and that made her cry aloud. Another time I saw her from the window and ran out to her. I told her she must take me with her. I cried and cried. She took my hand and walked with me a bit in the bazaar, buying me ice cream and sweets and a pinwheel. She promised to come and take me away as soon as she had her house settled, not knowing how difficult that would be. I was always watched closely by someone—a maid or my father. She wrote me letters which I never responded to and she knew my father must have ripped them up. Her only hope was that I would try to find her when I was older, but as time went by and she did not hear from me she grew afraid of me. Really afraid. That I would never want to see her, that if I did I might spit in her face or throw a rock at her.

13

Mahmood Majid came over in the middle of the week. He was out of his white uniform, and wore a plaid suit with small lapels, of obviously local material and make. His hair was slightly wet.

"How do you feel?" he asked immediately.

"Fine. I feel so much better already. I've hardly had any pain since I started the diet and the medication."

He sat down on the rug in the courtyard where my mother, uncle, and I were sitting, having tea. The samovar hissed and gave out tiny sparks.

"It's lucky we have that good X-ray machine now. I made them get it."

"We're all very grateful to you," my mother said, pouring some tea from the tea pot into a cup and adding water to it from the samovar. She put the cup and a saucer before Mahmood Majid.

Mahmood Majid talked to her and my uncle for a while, comfortably, as if he were related to them. Then he said to me, "I'd like to take you to a section that's historical. It has a mosque, a small shrine, a bazaar. Then we'll go to a restaurant in the bazaar and eat. But you have to wear a *chador* for the shrine, otherwise they won't let you in."

My mother gave me an extra *chador* she had, smiling at me as I put it on.

In the car I slipped off the *chador*. I'd put it back on when I needed it. He glanced at me and smiled. "Is that uncomfortable for you?"

"It feels very heavy on my head."

"If you wore it a few times you'd get used to it."

He turned on the radio. A woman was singing, her voice laden with passion—a song about the bittersweet miseries of love. Mahmood Majid became silent, looking entranced, listening to the song.

I tried to imagine making love to Mahmood Majid or falling in love with him. A barrier stood between us. He seemed like a brother to me, someone I knew too well deep down.

"Doesn't she have a beautiful voice?" he asked.

"I like it," I said. "When I first came here everything —even songs—seemed strange but that has been changing gradually."

"Of course things look different once you get used to them. I remember our conversation when I drove you to the hospital."

We passed a square, a tea house, surrounded by almond and cherry trees, a group of camels kneeling by a shed full of straw. Then, abruptly, we were outside of the town. There were scattered huts in the distance and ruins of old inns. We passed occasional cars. Men and women, travelling on donkeys, went by. Then a complex of buildings appeared inside a low clay wall.

"That's where we're going," he said.

I slipped the *chador* back on. He parked outside of the wall, where there were a few cars and buses, and led me inside.

Behind the wall people swarmed in doorways and on shady verandas. Several children had gathered under a tree with strings tied to its branches. The nasal drone of a Moslem priest filled the air.

We passed through a corridor and entered another courtyard where a simple beautiful mosque stood. I could see men and women lined up in separate chambers inside, praying.

"Do you want to join them?" Mahmood Majid whispered.

I shook my head.

"You never pray, do you?"

"No, do you?"

"I did even when I was in the United States. It makes you stop everything a few times a day, be alone with yourself."

"I wish I could pray," I said, believing it at the moment.

He began to give me a history of the place, how old everything was, the significance of each niche, dome, or decoration. I nodded.

"You're not listening to what I'm saying," he said, sounding slightly irritated.

"I'm looking. There are so many things to see."

"And there's so much more."

We went through more passageways and came out in front of the shrine with a gold dome and gold and mosaic decorations on its walls, all brilliant in sunlight.

We decided to go in and left our shoes with a man at

the door, receiving tickets for them. The several adjoining rooms inside were dim, lit only by a few candles. The wall around the sarcophagus of the saint and all the other walls were covered with silver circular knobs. People walked around, kissing the walls, whispering prayers and crying. Echoes, faraway, vibrated in my head, my whole body. Surges of memory, of going from chamber to chamber in mosques and shrines, clinging to my mother, flowed over the surface of my mind. Suddenly, in spite of myself, I stopped, leaned my head against a wall and kissed it, tears filling my eyes and rolling down my cheeks.

After the shrine we went to the bazaar to eat. Between arches on the ceiling there were occasional gaps, revealing the sky. A pale, late sun mottled the faces of the passers-by. Mahmood Majid stopped often to look at shops, a stairway leading to an ancient water storage tank, mosaics on doorways. He examined everything as though this were the first time he had been there. A few times he offered to buy something for me from a shop and I refused. We reached the restaurant he had in mind, tucked behind a little garden just outside of the bazaar.

We went to the second floor and sat by a window, overlooking the garden. The room had only a few tables, and except for several posters of local mosques, it was bare.

"They have excellent food here," Mahmood Majid said. "I know the waiter—I can tell him to go easy on spices for you."

"Good," I said. "This is a very pleasant place."

"I knew you'd like it."

The waiter came over and greeted him deferentially. After taking the order, the waiter left to come back with a tray of food—yogurt and cucumber, kebabs, rice, salad, and *doogh.*

"I'm sorry you can't eat everything," Mahmood Majid said. "If you're careful for a while the ulcer might go away."

"I thought they never go away completely."

"It could."

"It's odd that the symptoms were misplaced."

"It happens occasionally."

At the moment it did not seem to really matter that I had an ulcer. I selected some of the food and watched the sky darkening before the window as I ate.

"You know what I did when I first came back to Iran? I took a trip across the country, visiting mosque after mosque, shrine after shrine—I could never tire of them." He looked at me for a long moment as if to assess whether I approved. "I took my mother with me—she was very upset at the time. My nephew, her sister's son, had died in a car accident. There is a particularly nice shrine, of Saint Zobeideh, outside of Khasvin. It was very far from Teheran, where my mother lives, and my car broke down a couple of times on mud roads before we got to it. But with all the trouble it was worth it. There was no one there that day and we stayed for hours. Wild flowers grew around the grave and birds hopped around. It was so peaceful."

"I know what you mean—I felt some of that today, even with the crowd."

He chewed on his food, leaned forward a little and asked suddenly, "What's your husband like?"

The very thought of Tony brought back some of my anxiety—what had happened to him, why had he not answered my telegram? I was already ten days late getting back and he had not tried to contact me. I must try to call him that evening no matter how hard it might be.

"Oh, it's not easy to describe my husband," I said. "He's very American in many ways. He's from a middle-class family in the midwest, he's hard working and very rational."

I continued inwardly: but he's brittle, not so resilient and adaptable as you are. He doesn't have your open manner, your ability to ask question after question, to act overtly irritable or gay. Tony bottles things inside of him until they rot and begin to poison him.

"He couldn't be too typical, otherwise he wouldn't marry a foreign girl." He considered that for a moment and added, "Although you seem to have adopted his ways. You seem Americanized."

"Have you ever been married?" I asked.

"No, I haven't found the right person yet." He laughed. "I'm just hopelessly romantic. Do you mind if I order some wine. You won't be able to have much of it."

"Go ahead," I said. "But are they allowed to serve wine here?"

"They keep some for their regular customers. They bring it over in water jugs so that it won't be noticed."

He tapped on the table with his knuckles—the silver ring he wore made a rather loud sound. The waiter came. Mahmood Majid whispered his order although there was no one in the room. The waiter disappeared. He brought the wine over, looking sideways at me and conspiratorially at Mahmood Majid. He cleared the table and left.

"He obviously doesn't approve of a woman drinking," I

said, wondering to what extent Mahmood Majid himself approved.

"Oh, what does it matter?" he said. "You're here to have a good time."

He drank and I took some sips. The sun began to set, spreading pink, blue, and lavender across the sky. Then the colors disappeared quickly and the moon came out, standing behind a tall cypress.

A melancholy expression came over Mahmood Majid's face as he drank. I imagined him sighing a lot, listening to romantic songs as he grieved over the loss of someone he loved. I pictured him sitting and staring at the dark waters of a river with lines of poetry filling his mind. Suddenly the barrier I had felt between us was lifted and I wanted to be held by him, to touch him.

I looked into his eyes. I saw them melt into mine. I turned to the window and back to him. "Do you feel like taking a walk?" I asked.

He suggested going into the garden. The garden was wild and overgrown and full of a strong scent of unfamiliar flowers. Many of the plants were brownish from underwatering and heat.

We walked along a narrow path, in part covered by trees. The garden seemed to be built on the ruins of something. Through the trees I could see remains of a dome stuck to a wall, half of a stairway leading to nothing.

The path ended at a low wall. We stood there, side by side, and looked beyond it. Some huts were built randomly on a flat plane. Water flowed heavily in a gutter running among the huts. Except for the ripples of water and the occasional barks of a dog it was very quiet.

I turned my head slightly towards Mahmood Majid. He had been waiting for a signal. He put his hand on my back, caressing it.

We kissed for a long time, letting go and starting again. To be held tighter, closer, more intimately by this extremely nice man, to lie with him in his room, strewn with silk cushions, its walls decorated with Persian miniatures. Swimming with him in a secluded corner, like the boys we had seen on the road.

There were sounds of footsteps and simultaneously a voice saying, "Excuse me, Dr. Majid . . ."

We turned around. A man was standing there.

"We have to shut the gates. The restaurant closes at ten o'clock. I'm very sorry," he said.

I noticed for the first time that I had had the *chador* on all the time. Mahmood Majid's face seemed sheepish. All I wanted to do was to leave the garden as soon as possible.

"You saw us coming here?" Mahmood Majid asked in a daze.

"The waiter was looking for you and then he saw you walking this way."

"That's right, we didn't pay the bill," Mahmood Majid said.

In the car he was quiet. I became tense. The attraction I had felt towards him was destroyed. We talked very little all the way back. He took me to my mother's house without any hints of going to his house for a while. Perhaps he did have another woman—or maybe the fact that I was married inhibited him. He parked on the wider street near my mother's house and walked with me. At the door we stopped and faced each other.

His eyes seemed even darker than usual.

"I'll be seeing you again, I hope," he said, his voice rather formal.

"Yes, yes . . . of course." I said quickly and turned around to go.

The moon was immense above the courtyard, standing far away in the sky.

In the middle of the courtyard, I saw my mother coming out of her room and standing by the doorway.

"Oh, here you are," she said excitedly.

Another figure stood beside her. It was Tony.

14

He sat awkwardly on the rug in my room trying to keep his legs in a comfortable position as he ate the stew, rice, and salad my mother had put before him. I sat across from him. He looked a little older, his hair and shirt covered with dust from the bus ride. Even his dark blue valise and briefcase were dusty.

He had an obscure expression on his face—he always looked like that when he did not want to cope with an emotion openly. I could read his thoughts: what the hell are we doing here? Why aren't I back in my study with my familiar books, the soft leather chair I like to sit in so much, the spotlight that gives just the right amount of light? I must not say that to Feri though. She looks very edgy and, after all, no matter what she says, this is her home.

My telegram had never gotten to him. They might have phoned him while he was away (to a convention) and then thrown it away. He had decided to go to the convention because it was in San Francisco and since I was gone he thought he would turn a business trip into a little vacation. When I did not arrive at the time I was supposed to, he tried to phone me at my father's house but the operator could not find the number. He had begun to feel seriously worried as days went by.

"Then I got to your father's house and we couldn't understand each other," he said, trying to smile, but looking strained. "Finally your brother brought in someone from the neighborhood who knew English. They were very surprised to know that I was your husband. They had let me in, not knowing who I was or what I wanted."

"I'm sorry you had to get dragged away like this."

I told him about the letter of permission I needed to get out, my having gone to the hospital, how I went about finding my mother.

"Don't get so excited," he said after I told him about my mother. "It's nice but . . ."

That phrase, "Don't get excited," was a common phrase of his. He said it almost out of habit, but it often dulled the edge of excitement for me. I somehow resented it more than usual now.

"Your father sent you a note." He rummaged through his pockets. His shirt, pants, then the checkered sports jacket he had put at the edge of the bed. He found the note in the jacket and handed it to me.

I unfolded the yellow paper and began to read.

"My dear daughter, I went through so much trouble to find your mother's address so that I could give it to your husband. What's taking you so long? Your husband had to come all the way here to get you."

I smiled, reading my father's crooked and disorderly handwriting which had gotten worse in his old age.

My mother and uncle came in bringing tea and fruit,

and sat in a corner. My mother's face was mostly hidden behind her *chador*. I could see confusion reflected in her eyes. My uncle stared at Tony, a smile warming the immobility of his posture as he sat stiffly on crossed legs. They tried to talk to Tony through me and he tried to talk to them, but a silence lingered behind the voices. Everything seemed in slow motion again as it had when I first arrived in Iran.

"It's late. We'd better let you sleep," my mother said. "I heated the water if he wants to take a shower." Then she and my uncle left the room quietly, the way they had entered it, as if it no longer belonged to them.

Tony took a shower quickly—in an area off the room, a patched-up stall added on later, not much more comfortable than the one in my father's house. Then we went to bed, which was barely large enough for both of us.

"Sleeping here is like camping out," he said.

The window revealed a sky crammed with stars.

"That's right," I said.

His hand was on my breast, his mouth on the side of my face, but we were strange with each other.

"You're different. I'll have to pluck you away before you become too comfortable here, he said."

He removed his hand from me and faced the ceiling.

"What's bothering you?" I asked.

"Nothing." Then he said, "I had to leave my work and come all the way here. I left so many things in the middle. Do you know, they gave me a class of one hundred students to teach next semester?" A bitterness had come into his tone.

What would he be like in a few years if some of his expectations for himself failed? He would be like those colleagues of mine or his who always felt put upon by the world, begrudging the success of anyone who did better than themselves. And what if I became like that?

"You don't care about my troubles. You're only worried about your work," I said.

"No? Why did I come all the way here then?"

"It's just that I wish we didn't worry about work all the time."

"It's easy for you to say that. You're a woman. There isn't as much pressure on you to produce."

"There must have been some pressure. I have an ulcer."

"What?"

"An ulcer. That's why I was in the hospital."

"I assumed you had a virus." He seemed as surprised as I was when I found out about the ulcer. He raised himself to his elbow and, staring at my face, said, "Are you sure the doctors here know what they're talking about?"

"It showed on the X-ray."

"That's hard to believe. Now you have to eat all that boring food you don't like."

"I know."

"How do you feel now?"

"O.K. The pain was mostly in my back and chest, instead of my stomach."

"Then, they might have made a mistake," he said, his voice becoming lively.

"No. The pain went away immediately with the new diet."

"Where were you this evening?" he asked.

"I went out to a restaurant."

"By yourself?"

"No, with the doctor who took care of me."

"Oh," he said, putting his hands under his head. "Is that why you've been hanging around here? You obviously weren't in a rush to come back."

"You know that's not why—I had to stay."

He pulled the blanket over his head.

"Tony," I said after a moment.

He did not reply.

15

I lay awake, thinking about Tony as if he were still far away. Indeed in that short period of separation I had grown more apart from him than I would have believed possible.

I thought of what it was like when I had just met him. A white light had begun to shine on things so that everything seemed extraordinarily bright. In that blinding light I almost totally submitted to him, letting him lead me, seeing things through his eyes.

Before meeting him I was lost and confused. I had not been prepared for the small girls' college near Boston. Life in the dormitory with its long, gray walls and uniform rooms, students wearing lipstick and walking around the halls with curlers in their hair. The midnight fire alarm when the entire student body swarmed into the street, the mixers with nearby boys' schools, the swings under the trees where students sat with their dates, holding hands or kissing, the beauty contests, the prayers before meals in the large dining room, the compulsory church and Vespers, masklike faces that smiled and talked to me but really said nothing, the voices, monotonous, meaningless, the English language itself. . . .

The houses were identical, their doors closed, with no

children playing in the street. Everyone rode past in cars with windows up. I thought there was nothing really interesting about the country and no one seemed to be enjoying himself. Everyone in cars, everything wrapped within something else.

I skipped classes whenever I could. I lay in bed in my room, looking at the rows of trees in the yard or the leaves falling, aware of something important dissolving. I became empty of everything except for the thin, frail threads of the past. The bell announcing classes or mealtimes jarred my nerves. Now it is time to get up, dress, walk, talk, eat. Now it is getting dark. There are rapid footsteps in the hall, whispers. The long night is ahead of me. I would listen to a clock I had brought with me. It ticked the way it had in my room at home.

After a semester the foreign student adviser called me into her office. She flushed with restrained anger as she spoke, "I know there have been cultural adjustments for you but you have to make more of an attempt. If your grades don't pick up. . . ."

I began to study nonstop.

I met Louise in a biology course. She was from the South and was very thin and pale, with huge blue eyes and brown hair that she wore straight down her back. She stopped by my room every day at supper time to go to the dining room. We began to study together and, on Saturday nights, when everyone went on dates, she and I stayed in the dormitory and talked. Her major was art to which she devoted herself passionately. She began to confide in me that she had never had a menstrual period, that her breasts were no larger than coins and she wore padded bras, that her parents were disturbed that she never went out on dates. Later she told me she was in love with one of the art instructors. The instructor was tall, blond, wore a wedding ring, and walked around with a grin on his face. I asked her what she liked about him. She said, "Oh, he's so brilliant. He's the brightest man I've ever met." She was not sure how to get his attention. She knew he read late into the night in the library of the art department. But that building was closed to students after six. She decided to hide in a closet until the janitor left and then come out and try to talk to the instructor.

After that she would disappear one or two nights a week into the art department. I was envious of these nocturnal visits.

When Christmas came she stayed in Boston and her brother Jim came to visit her. He looked very much like her, except for his expression which was tense, and he talked all the time with his lips close together. One night, when Louise went to the art department again, he and I went to a movie and then to a drive-in restaurant. We ate hamburgers, french fries and milk shakes. His father was a successful broker and wanted Jim to share the business with him once he got out of college. He and Louise, he said, were considered rebels by everyone—for instance no one he knew in his hometown would date a girl from a foreign country. He squeezed my hand to make sure I was not offended. We drove to a dark street overlooking the Charles River and we kissed. "You're very pretty," he said.

Around noon the next day, Louise came to my room. She had pulled her hair back into a bun.

"I like your brother," I said.

"You have to be careful with him."

"What do you mean?"

"Oh, he has delusions of grandeur." Then she said, "I

wonder what it would be like to do it all the way with a boy."

"I'd be afraid."

Her expression grew sad. I noticed that she was pale, her eyes bloodshot.

"What's the matter?" I asked.

"Nothing."

Two or three days before the end of the holiday, Jim took me to a nightclub where jazz was played. We sat in a booth in a dark corner and talked and drank wine.

"Have you ever drunk wine before?" he asked.

"No."

"Well, you have a lot to learn." He laughed but there was an edge to his voice.

"You know I don't really want to get involved with anyone, not in a real way. Once I almost killed myself over a Mexican girl. I was in love with her and wanted to marry her but of course that was out of the question. My father threatened to cut off money for my education. I would have gone ahead and married her anyway but her parents also forbade her to see me."

"And that was the end?"

"One night we met secretly. It was a beautiful night. We hugged each other for hours, not saying anything, but both of us crying."

"Well, that's too bad."

"Is that all you can say?"

"What else is there to say?"

He became sullen. I watched his face in the twilight-red of the restaurant—it seemed troubled. He drove me back to the campus, remaining sullen all the way.

When we reached the dormitory he stopped the car without turning off the engine and I got out.

I saw him once more. He was sitting in Louise's room when I came in. I was about to leave but she insisted I should stay. Attempts at conversation fell flat and I found my eyes clinging to items in the room for something meaningful. Gauze curtains, a checkered bedspread, brown furniture—the same things found in every room.

After a few moments I got up and left. Out in the hall I heard Louise saying, "Well, she's from a different culture."

I did not hear Jim's response or what he had said to provoke Louise's remark. I went into my room and cried. Louise and I were never the same with each other again.

My new friendships were never as rewarding as the one with Louise had been originally. But then, doing well at school became my object. Biology began to fascinate me; the subtle and complicated interplay of cells—dying, reproducing—or the way drugs could make changes in the development of an organism.

During the summers I worked: twice as a file clerk in an office in a hospital, once doing research for a biologist.

In the summer, right after graduating, I met Tony. I had a job as a research assistant to a psychologist at a university in Cambridge, where I would start graduate work the following year.

The office was off a long corridor with many small rooms and laboratories, mostly wired for pigeon and rat experiments. The sound of pigeons pecking and rats pressing levers echoed along the corridor like a clock gone haywire.

In the afternoon the office would be crowded with students and other faculty members who came to talk to my boss. I would sit quietly.

Then one afternoon Tony came in and took a seat. My boss was away and he sat there waiting, impatiently tapping the desk with his fingers.

"Do you know when he's coming back?" he asked me after a while.

"He should be back any minute."

"Are you a student here?" he asked in an offhand way.

"I will be next year. And you?"

"I'm in urban planning. I want to talk to your boss about crowding, about how many people can occupy a certain space without going berserk."

"That would be interesting to know," I said awkwardly.

"Where are you from?"

"Iran."

"It used to be called Persia. I liked that name better. It fits with my image of the place."

"What's your image?"

"Gardens springing up in the midst of deserts, magic carpets, caravans jingling in the night, and dark-eyed girls behind veils."

"Not too bad," I said.

He got up abruptly and went towards the door. "I wonder if he's coming back."

"Sometimes he just disappears like that."

He went out and returned in a moment. "I've a request to make."

"What?"

"I'm invited to a party tonight. Would you like to go with me?"

I was surprised and I hesitated.

"We don't have to go to the party if you don't want to."

"Yes," I said quickly before he would change his mind. "I'll go to the party."

He left and I sat there, suddenly in a state of euphoria.

His eyes were so blue.

It was the blueness of his eyes, changeable, glinting like glass held against light, his blond hair, that cool way about him. He was so different from me, from all the men I had known while I was growing up.

The night I slept with him for the first time, we went for a walk along the Charles River, where other men and women strolled or reclined on the grass. The air was warm, carrying the nostalgia of early autumn.

Holding hands, we walked away from the grassy bank of the river towards a darker section and then into a narrow street.

In the middle of the street Tony pointed to a gray building and said, "That's where I live. I have a small apartment—one room and a bathroom."

"It's a nice building," I said and added hesitantly, "I'd like to see it."

We went inside. He poured wine into glasses and gave one to me. He took out slices of dark bread from the refrigerator, cut them into small squares, and put them on a plate. Then he took out some cheese and put it on another plate, doing all this carefully, shaping everything into designs, making sure nothing remained with jagged, imperfect edges.

The same neatness dominated the apartment with its well-arranged furniture. Books and records lined one of the walls from floor to ceiling. The other walls were covered with burlap. A partition separated an area from the rest of the room to form the kitchen.

He put some records on the phonograph and we sat on the wide sofa with immense bolsters. We drank the wine and talked. He kissed me lightly a few times. Then he turned off the light and we lay together on the sofa.

"It's nice to hold you like this," he said, not quite letting go of himself. Even in the dark, I kept thinking of his looks, the blondness, the coolness.

"Is this your first time?" he asked.

"Yes."

"Well . . ." He got up, went to the bathroom and came back. "We have to be careful. You don't want to get pregnant."

When I was younger my head had been filled with stories of women losing their virginity, the pain, the humiliation and final abandonment by the men . . . but what I felt now was a kind of lightness, as though I would float away.

As I felt him becoming hard and soft, and the chill that followed as he tried to enter and failed, and tried again and finally pulled away and said, "It's not going to work," I was left with a sense of confusion. Maybe he did not like me enough. Maybe I had done something wrong. I waited for him to speak.

"I know it's silly but I feel I'd be taking advantage of you," he said.

"Advantage!"

"It's just that . . . that it's your first time."

"But . . ."

He patted me affectionately. "You'll come back here again and we'll do it right then."

He got up, put on another record and lay beside me again. We were quiet for a while.

"What are you thinking about?" I asked.

"Oh, just that this evening you're with me."

"Every night after you leave me I feel lost—I've been having bad dreams."

"What do you dream?"

"They're frightening dreams, but I never remember them."

"Too bad."

"Do you dream much?"

"Either I don't dream or I don't remember them."

"You're so peaceful." Suddenly miserable, I pressed my head against his chest. "Tell me how to be so calm, how to stop worrying about everything."

"Maybe I'm not so calm and rational as I seem—I certainly didn't perform very well tonight."

He began to caress me again. He was suddenly vigorous, forceful. I felt his skin, heard his hard breathing, as I came in and out of consciousness, lost in him.

He took me to Urbana, Illinois, to meet his parents. The television went on and on, giving out a numbing drone. It was a large house with beige wall-to-wall carpeting, furnished mostly in walnut. Pictures of shipwrecks and landscapes decorated the walls. No doors banged shut loudly, no footsteps were heard. It snowed, white flakes falling steadily before picture windows, covering the evergreens, the parked cars on the street, the pavement, muffling sounds.

His father was an engineer, a quiet withdrawn man who would lose interest in conversation quickly, then turn to the television screen. His mother spent hours cooking pies and roasts, watching a smaller television in the kitchen. They both had blond hair and Tony's delicate features.

Whereas his father was extremely calm, his mother often appeared agitated, dropping a dish or banging a spatula against the kitchen counter. She asked me questions that made me uncomfortable. "Your family must be proud that you've come to America and done so well," or "Tony has always liked the unusual."

She attended church regularly. Her husband preferred to spend the time working on his model airplanes in the basement. Tony had rarely gone even when a child. He had been thin, serious, the kind of boy who got involved for hours in a project. His mother had to remind him to eat or sleep.

At night, lying in bed with Tony, I felt protected by the erotic current enveloping us. We talked, holding each other closely.

"It's almost spring and it's still snowing," he said.

"I know. I love to see the snow this late in the year."

"Soon we'll be married."

"Yes."

"I never thought I'd get married until I met you. It always seemed like too much of a commitment."

"You've known a lot of women."

"None of them were like you. You don't seem to have any expectations about marriage."

He was right—I had no domestic skills, no ideas of how to handle money, or life with a man.

I had so much to learn from him. The names of kitchen items and foods that had slipped by me in the college years when I had lived in the dormitory, what brands to shop for, how to budget money—we were both on small fellowships. Other things besides: how to write a good paper, how to finish a test quickly, how to organize my time.

I began to live for his coming and going, submitting myself helplessly to him, keeping nothing back. In so many ways he was the opposite of me. His ease with women. The lack of complications and mysteries about his past—his family life indicated an effortless, uneventful upbringing. His unquestioned sense of belonging to his own culture. He was gentle, charming, and yet I was full of an anxiety that somehow I did not have a firm hold on him. He might abandon me without explanation, or die, or just disappear. Even with him in the room, in bed with me, I suffered fear of loss.

I would ask over and over, "Do you love me?"

"I married you, didn't I?"

"I want you to say so anyway."

"I love you."

I clung to him. "I'm so afraid I'll lose you."

"But that would mean I'd lose you too."

"Don't say that." I covered his lips with my fingers.

Later he said, "I married you because you're far away from home, without a tangible past."

"So that you can make me to your own image?"

More and more I tried to be like him, like his world, fighting memories.

16

In the morning I got up before Tony and went into the courtyard to wash. My uncle was standing by a walnut tree, shaking it. An orange cat had climbed up the tree and was looking down, mewing.

"I'm trying to get him to come down," my uncle said. "He's afraid to do it on his own."

"I've never seen him before."

"He comes and goes. He catches a lot of the mice here."

"Where's my mother?" I asked.

"She went to the mosque. She went to pray for you. She's afraid you'll be leaving soon." He smiled as if to counteract his own somber tone. "Was your husband comfortable last night?"

"He seemed to be. He slept well."

Tony came out and stood by the doorway.

"Come here and wash," I said, pointing to the pool.

He walked to the pool, rubbing his eyes.

"What a wreck this place is," he said. In daylight he seemed to have forgotten his anger at me, and his tone was gentle. "At one time it must have been beautiful—look at the mosaic on the walls, the shape of the courtyard. It would be nice to reconstruct the whole place again."

"It'd be a big project," I said.

He leaned awkwardly over the pool, washing his hands and face under the faucet. The sun glinted on his hair.

I handed him the towel I had used and he dried himself.

The cat jumped onto a lower branch, then to the ground, and began to run away.

Tony and I went back into the room and Tony shaved without water. That left scratches on his face.

My uncle came in carrying the breakfast tray—bread, cheese, butter, milk, and tea.

"Why don't you stay and eat with us?" I asked my uncle.

"I've already eaten but I'll sit with you for a moment." He sat down on crossed legs. "Are you going to show your husband around today?"

"Yes, I think so."

"Tell him how happy we are to have you here."

I said that to Tony. "Tell him I understand," he said.

My mother came in, smelling of rosewater she had put on in the mosque. "You slept late," she said. "That was good. Your husband must have been tired." Her face had the same tight, almost shocked expression as it had when I first saw her.

From under her *chador* she brought out the photograph of me as a little girl. "Tell him I saved this."

Tony took the picture from her and examined it. "You looked a lot like you do now."

My mother pointed to the rose in the picture. "You used to love flowers. You'd come into the yard every day and inspect the bushes for new blossoms, new leaves. There was the stump of a huge tree and you would sit on it, surrounded by flowers, and play for hours. You loved birds too and I bought you a parrot once. You'd sit and talk to it for a long time. I took the bird with me when I left and spoke to it. It was like talking to you. And one day when the bird died I wept and wept over it."

Beneath her overt display of emotion I could see shadows of pain stretching inward.

"Every morning when I woke, I thought, she will be eating breakfast now, she's in the courtyard playing now, and later I said, she's grown up, she'll get married soon."

Tony had leaned forward, staring at her, but he spoke to me. "She looks sad. Does she know we're leaving?"

"I think so." I saw the scene with precision: my mother and I saying goodbye—embraces, write soon, I will, I will, tears. Then the images blurred. The picture of Lexington had grown darker and darker. The courtyard before me was full of sun, real. The smell of rosewater lingered in the room.

"We must leave on the next bus," Tony said, tapping the wall with his hand. A powdery stuff came off and settled on his shirt. He began to wipe it away.

"You've come halfway around the world and you don't want to see anything?"

"I do. In fact I like this town. It must have been laid out a thousand years ago and it still functions. But we have to get back. I've left my work in the middle and you've already missed so many days."

"Still, it's crazy to run off like this."

I went to the window, turning away from him. How was I going to explain anything to him, the change in me?

"I'm not going back now," I said. "Not for a while."

"What, what for? Your job is already in jeopardy. They aren't going to hold it for you forever."

"I'm not sure if I want that job. I don't think I'm cut out for it. I might want to do something different altogether."

"All of a sudden?"

"I've been thinking about it."

He began to put a few things back into his suitcase. "It's the doctor, isn't it?" He did not look at me. I could see anger tightening the muscles of his face.

"You know it isn't," I said vehemently.

"Then what are you going to do here? I don't understand it. You didn't want to come back for years and now suddenly you don't want to leave. It doesn't make sense."

"It's just that . . . I have a lot of catching up to do."

"Well, do what you want. I'm telling you what's good for you. The rest is up to you. I can't drag you back. You aren't a child, even though you're acting like one."

I felt exasperated, angry, helpless. Then panicky as I saw him shutting his suitcase, determined and ready to leave at any minute. I could not trust my own emotions under the circumstances. Perhaps I was brainwashed, magnifying my problems with him and at work. Perhaps the distance I felt between us was exaggerated in that environment, not quite real.

I began to cry. "I can't bear this."

"This is all very silly."

"I've been selfish to completely forget about my mother, not even try to find her all those years, see what's going on with her."

"It's she who left you, abandoned you. She's the one who didn't try hard enough to get you back." His voice softened a little.

"How could she really, under the circumstances?" I kept crying.

"You're feeling guilty because you found her in the state she's in, basically alone and destitute. If she were happy and well settled you wouldn't think of it." He came over to me and caressed my arm, trying to console me. "What you could do is give her some money. Maybe send her some every month."

"I offered to help but she refused. I said I'd buy her a house but she said she likes this place."

"Just send her the money and come and visit her again."

He was so reasonable and understanding.

Perhaps I was trying to escape into the easy emotional comfort of childhood. Only a month ago everything in Iran had seemed nightmarish. My doubts piled up more and more. How odd my staying would seem to those who knew me in the United States. What impulse, they would ask, could lead a woman like her to abandon her career and stay on in a place she professed to have left behind, a place whose values she had outgrown, where the attitude towards women remains so primitive?

I wiped my tears with a handkerchief and began to pack.

"Hurry up," Tony said, walking ahead of me through a wide open area with an ancient crumbling bridge on one side and some huts on the other.

"You stop hurrying. This is as fast as I can go." The lace on one of my sandals kept coming loose.

"You always lag behind me."

"You always walk ahead of me."

He stopped for a moment. "Is this your Iranian upbringing, to always walk behind a man?"

He was trying to joke but I could see he was tense, as he always was when away from work for any length of time.

I caught up with him.

"What was your mother saying to you before we left?"

"The usual kind of thing—that I should write to her and come for a visit soon."

My mother and uncle had acted surprisingly serene when we said goodbye. They kissed me and shook hands with Tony. He smiled at them politely.

Through the lattice beneath the bridges I could see people sitting by a stream, picnicking. They ate, washed dishes, or reclined on cloths they had spread out. Children were swinging on ropes tied to trees.

"I'm going to take some pictures here," Tony said. "That bridge is interesting. Look at the intricate lattice supporting it." We went closer to the bridge. "I wish I had more time to study this town. I can't get over how ancient it is and how these people just sit around its ruins."

"It gives you an odd sensation, doesn't it?" I said.

He adjusted the camera. Children began to collect, one by one, in its area of focus. "Look at them," he said, clicking a few times.

He slung the camera on his shoulder and we walked away. The children continued watching us, squinting in the sun.

We walked a while longer on the barren land and then went through a succession of narrow alleys, coming out into a wide street, lined with elegant mansion-like houses with wooden or iron doors. A man sat against a wall in the lotus position, his lips moving as he passed a rosary through his fingers. He seemed oblivious of us and his surroundings.

Then we came upon an historic garden which I knew held a famous bath inside. A premier had been murdered in the bath. Four men had come in and cut his veins while he was relaxing in the warm water. I recounted the story to Tony as we walked through the garden and the bath.

It was getting near the departure time of the bus and we began to head towards the station. We bought our tickets and then stopped in a small shop next to the booth, where leather goods and jewelry were displayed. Tony bought a silver ring with an oval carnelian on it and put it on. I bought a leather pocketbook.

The bus arrived on time. It was not as crowded as it had been when I came to Kashan. I let Tony sit by the window and I sat beside him. He began to read almost immediately.

Again the same monotonous land, broiling sky, and broken-down remnants of another civilization. A hot wind blew in through the windows. Our hair was ruffled and our faces covered with a thin layer of salt-dust. The seat became moist and sticky.

Tony kept shifting his feet. Once he got up to shake his legs. "I'm getting cramps," he said. "This ride is endless."

"I know, and to do it two days in a row. We should have stayed at least another day in Kashan. It was crazy to leave in such a rush."

He turned to his book and did not respond. After a moment he put his arm around me and said, "You should take it easy when we get back. Ulcers can become dangerous, as you know."

"If I can take it easy."

"We should make a new schedule for ourselves."

"I guess we could try."

A woman sitting in front of us asked me if Tony was an American. She was pleasant, smiling, but I said curtly, "Yes," and turned away. I felt a sadness, aware that something was lost between Tony and me and I had to work hard to get it back.

17

My father acted a bit sulky when Tony and I returned, but became more talkative as the evening wore on. He studiously avoided any mention of my mother. Nor did he try to discuss my going back to the States now that Tony was here. I told him about going to the hospital and my ulcer. He said, "That comes from worrying too much." His tone implied "I told you so." I shrugged, not wanting to pursue the subject.

Tony and I spent the next morning buying tickets—two days later was the first date available—and getting my exit visa.

In the afternoon Darius came to the doorway of my room and said, "I'll take you for a ride if you want."

I asked Tony if he wanted to go. He was sitting on the bed, looking over a paper he had a deadline on in a few days.

"I don't know. I thought I'd finish this first." Then he changed his mind. "All right, I'll go."

My father and Ziba were sitting in the courtyard, sipping tea.

"Darius is taking us for a ride," I said. "Would you like to come?"

"Neither of us likes rides." My father's face looked deeply wrinkled in the bright sun. He patted Ziba on the back. "Right?"

Ziba nodded and rubbed her head against his hand.

The display of affection between them startled me. I had either neglected to see it before or they felt more free now to be open about it in front of me.

"Tell him we have some of the best sights," my father said, looking at Tony. "Tell him we invented many things that the world uses."

I said that to Tony. He nodded at my father.

"Show him Shemiran, the Zoor Khaneh," Ziba said to Darius, her eyes fixed on Tony.

No one referred to him by his name.

We started to leave—Darius walked a little ahead of us, carrying his jacket over his shoulder.

In the car I sat in the middle and kept telling Darius to be more cautious. He drove frantically, as did most of the other drivers, and Tony and I clutched one another at each turn, each jerk of the car.

We drove through the center of Teheran and then entered the wide, quiet streets leading to Shemiran.

Darius pointed to the Western-looking shops and restaurants. "Make sure he takes a good look at these," he said. "Shall we eat in one of those restaurants?"

"They aren't interesting to him. They're like restaurants in the United States."

"Then I know where to take him."

We passed through the Shemiran Bridge, jammed with pedestrians, vendors, cars, pushcarts heaped with pyramids of grapes, apples and oranges, fresh gold dates, green almonds, bunches of bananas, pomegranates. Plastic bags, belts, and jewelry. Toy camels. Noise vibrated in the air.

"What's going on here?" Tony asked. "Something

seems to be happening."

"This is just the usual crowd, people come here in the evening and walk around."

"Unbelievable."

For the first time since he had arrived he seemed somewhat relaxed. It made me feel better.

We turned on to a quiet, uphill road. Then Darius parked the car and we got out. We walked on the narrow hilly paths, then down a slope. A man selling green almonds from a wooden platter on his head approached us. Darius stopped him and bought three bags of almonds. We ate the sour fruit, spitting out the pits as we walked. At the bottom of the slope there was a restaurant. Its sitting area consisted of rug-covered platforms over a rivulet of water. People sat on the rugs, eating food from trays laid in front of them. Gas lamps, hung on cypress and oak trees, provided a flickering yellow light. A cool, wet breeze rose from the water and brushed against me.

We sat on a platform too and a waiter came over, hopping over the stream. Darius ordered the usual things, *chelo kebab*, yogurt and cucumber, radishes, *doogh*. He leaned back on one elbow, looking around at the other customers.

When the food came Tony took a bite and said, "I can't eat this, my stomach feels funny."

"Maybe it's from those almonds," I said.

"Doesn't he like it? Shall I order something else?" Darius viewed Tony with hurt eyes. He pushed the rice and the kebab towards Tony and said, "Good, good."

Tony pointed to his stomach.

"He's a little sick," I said.

"Does he want a beer?"

Tony said yes, he did.

Darius and I ate the food while Tony sipped the beer.

"See that chenar tree?" Darius said, pointing to a hollow tree about six feet in diameter, off the road. "An old man lives in it. He just sits there most of the time and meditates. Children come and talk with him or harass him but he just roosts there like a bird."

"What does he do in the winter?"

"He wraps a thick sheepskin coat around him—anyway he has the protection of the tree. He's probably up there right now, looking out. Sometimes I wish I could do that, get away from everyone—Ziba, father—and be on my own completely."

"Why don't you move out and get a place of your own?"

"Ziba would kill herself if I just moved out." His face became a little wistful. "Sometimes I wish I could travel, see the world, like you have."

"What's stopping you?"

"Obligations, maybe laziness." He sighed. "Life!"

"Life is what you make it to be," I said.

"As if any of us could choose anything."

"You want to spend the rest of your life living the way you are now?"

He shrugged. "This is just philosophical talk."

"What are you discussing so seriously?" Tony asked.

"Nothing specific."

"The least you could do is translate."

"I *have* been translating most of the time." My words sounded more abrupt than I had meant them to be.

He became sullen. Then he said, "You know I don't like to travel. You could try to be more pleasant."

"Is something wrong?" Darius asked.

"No," I said, and fell into silence. After a while I turned

to Tony, "You've been ruining everything for me since you came here."

"I'm sorry."

"Shall we leave?" Darius asked, sensing the argument.

"That's a good idea," I said.

Darius signalled to the waiter to bring the check. Then he said, unexpectedly, "It must be hard to live with someone who doesn't know your language. He doesn't even pronounce your name right."

"I don't think these things matter." I sounded defensive, I knew.

"When the gap between two people is too deep it can drown each of them." He made a descriptive gesture with his hands.

I saw a gap and myself drowning in it.

The waiter came over. Darius insisted on paying, and we left.

Up the road two little girls were standing by the doorway of a house, bouncing a rubber ball back and forth between them. A young boy and a girl stood behind a lamppost kissing. Two men walked slowly behind us. They whispered something to each other and laughed.

Darius turned around and said to the men, "Are you asking for trouble?"

"What's the matter?" I asked.

He ignored me.

"Look at him, he thinks he's a big shot," one of the men said.

Darius stood in front of them, blocking their way. The two men passed by him and quickly got into a red car. One of them was dark, thin, with a long face and tiny eyes. The other was fat, with his belly bulging out above his belt.

Darius began to follow them. I took his arm and tried to pull him away. "Come on, let's go."

"Get into the car," he said to me, his eyes still fixed on the men.

"What's going on?" Tony asked.

"I think those men said something about me that insulted Darius. The same thing happened once in a restaurant."

"Pretty macho, isn't he?"

The two of us got into the car. Darius threw a long, warning look towards the red car and got in too.

The two men had started the engine of their car and as they were about to pull away one of them shouted, "She sells herself to that American." He let out a shrill laugh.

Darius began to follow their car.

"For God's sake we're going to get killed," Tony said, sitting back tensely.

"Darius, please."

He was pale and the veins on his neck stood out.

"Tell him to let us out of the car," Tony said.

"Stop, stop," I said to Darius.

Darius's eyelids fluttered and he breathed noisily, in sucks. Then he rammed our car into the back of theirs. The red car suddenly jerked forward and began to move very fast, its back dented in. Darius tried to pursue them but finally he slowed down. "I could have killed them," he whispered.

"He's crazy," Tony said to me. "We almost got killed.

"That's the way he thinks he should act."

After a moment, through the mirror, I could see the red car with the two men behind us.

"Look, they're following *us*," I told Darius.

"They're hoping to get even with me."

At an intersection with several crossing streets he suddenly turned the car around and drove speedily through a narrow lane.

"They will never find us now," he said.

"We'll be lucky if we survive this," Tony mumbled, shaking his head.

We were quiet the rest of the way back.

18

"I'm afraid I just don't like your brother. Have you really looked at him, at his eyes, the way he holds his shoulders?" Tony said in bed that night.

"He's volatile."

He hugged me. "I think the problem is that we haven't screwed for a long time, since you left for this trip."

We touched, but mechanically. All the sensations of being close to him were there—the warmth of his skin, his breath, the curve of his thighs, but something was missing at the core of it all. I thought of Mahmood Majid, the abortive physical contact between us, leading to nothing. Perhaps he would be an adequate substitute for whatever it was I yearned for if he were with me in bed instead of Tony.

Tony pulled away from me.

"What's the matter?" I asked.

"Your attitude bothers me."

"I don't understand," I said, like a child trying to hide her guilt.

"You just lie there passively and expect me to do everything."

"I'm sorry. Shall we try again?"

"Never mind. I can wait." He turned around, facing the wall.

"I guess I'm just not myself," I said, putting my arm around him.

He turned to me again. "Do you want to do it?"

"O.K."

The sex, all the way through, was as mechanical as our preliminary touches.

Again I stayed awake and he fell asleep immediately.

After a while I got out of bed, went into the courtyard and sat on the steps leading up to the porch. The clouds moved over the moon but there was no wind. Some of the pomegranates had cracked open, revealing the glistening seeds inside. A black cat with bright yellow eyes jumped down from a doorway and stared at me. Then I became aware of a shadow, coming closer. I turned around—it was my father.

"You had a hard time sleeping too?" he asked. "You were always like this, restless."

"I know."

"Remember how you used to crawl into my bed for comfort?"

"Yes."

We were both whispering.

"Tell me," he said. "Do you think you're doing the right thing rushing back?"

"No, I don't."

"Stay a little longer. We'll try not to bother you."

"I don't know if I can," I said hesitantly.

He shook his head.

"How was your mother?" he asked, at last.

"She was fine, I guess."

His eyes were on me, wide-open, hurt. His shadow fell starkly against the ground. It seemed to me that once long ago we had stood in this same spot in the dark and talked.

"Don't you understand the disgrace she brought on me? For a long time after she left me I went around with my head bent, afraid to see anyone. Faces seemed to come out of the walls, laughing at me, shouting, 'You fool!' And I had given her no reason for that. I had always indulged her." His voice failed him for an instant. Then he went on. "I wonder if she wasn't possessed by something beyond her will, beyond common sense, that made her destroy herself and all those around her."

"I know how you must have felt," I said. "In a way I felt the same when she left."

"You would have grown up differently if she hadn't left. You'd be proud of your country, your family." He breathed heavily and then he went on. "You wouldn't get that awful stomach wound you have."

There was a slight pain just then in my stomach, in the right place for the first time. I had a vision of it growing bigger and bigger, becoming lacerated and bleeding, covering my whole inside.

"Who knows why I got that," I said, trying to brush aside the self-pity that came over me.

"Last week I dreamed of a letter that you had sent to me. There was something in the letter that made me cry. When I didn't actually get it the next day I went to the post office to inquire about it." He paused, looked at me intently and added, "The post office had burnt down. All the letters, all the packages people had sent to each other were destroyed." His eyes darted around nervously as if he were watching the flames.

"Well, I didn't send you a letter," I said.

He seemed not to be listening to me. "And now you'll be disappearing once again into that tunnel you've dug for yourself." He looked stricken, even afraid. I reached out and touched his arm. This was the first time since I came that I had touched him voluntarily. The contact reverberated with some of the love I had for him as a child.

At my touch he reached forward and kissed me quickly on the cheek.

"Go to sleep now," he said, looking up at the sky. "Soon it will be dawn."

There was a soft, moist quality to the air. We walked together for a few feet and then we each went to our rooms.

I crept back into bed, not even trying to sleep. I rolled my head from side to side on the pillow, aching with irresolution, as I used to when I was frustrated or angry as a child. Now, as then, this thrashing of the head solved nothing.

I understood what provoked suicide—people taking overdoses of sleeping pills or jumping out of windows. Perhaps they too lay awake in the middle of the night, with their identity and sense of belonging suddenly reversed or blurred.

19

Darius seemed to be in a good mood the next morning. He was whistling a sentimental tune as he squatted near the doorway to his room, polishing his shoes.

I watched him from my room and then went into the courtyard, leaving Tony behind. I could hear the clatter of dishes, and water running in the kitchen.

"Come here and look at something," Darius called to me. He had on a saffron-colored shirt and blue jeans, both tight-fitting. His hair was combed and oiled, and stood in a high pompadour.

He pointed to a framed picture on his wall. "If you like it I'll give it to you as a going-away present."

I looked at the painting. It was a miniature I had seen once before of a man and a woman lying together in an embrace under a sheet on a mattress, their heads on a plump, oval-shaped pillow. Their shoes lay neatly side by side next to the bed. It was all done in exquisite colors of gold, red, and violet. Underneath the painting was a grama-phone. Some records—a few of them with bright yellow covers—were stacked beside it. On the floor there was a rug with paisley designs. I had not seen Darius's room since I had returned home.

"It's a beautiful picture," I said.

"I knew it's the kind of thing you'd like." He put down the cloth, which was covered with shoe wax, picked up another cloth, and began to shine the shoes.

Ziba came to the kitchen doorway, unwrapped her *chador* which she had tied to her waist and put it back on her head. She smoothed it down carefully on the sides and then entered the courtyard. Her lips looked a little pinched at seeing me. Then she forced a smile.

"You look very tired," she said to me.

"I haven't been getting much sleep," I said.

"Where are you going?" Darius asked her.

"Where else? Shopping for food while my big son polishes and repolishes his shoes. You should be ashamed." Her voice was light.

Darius chuckled as she passed him. He put his shoes neatly together like the ones in the picture.

"Your husband doesn't like me, does he?" he said.

"Why do you always act so belligerent? You almost crashed into that car."

"It was him—your husband—the way he seemed to be judging me that got me worked up." He sat on crossed legs and looked at his hands.

I could see he had bitten his nails.

There was a loud knock at the door. Darius listened carefully.

"Who could that be—the door is open," he said.

There was another loud knock. Darius went to the door. I heard a conversation going on between him and someone else. Silence followed, and then the sound of footsteps going away.

I waited in the courtyard, thinking of Darius. The anger

he dispersed randomly, I kept inside, under tight control.

A long time had passed since Darius left. I went outside and looked up and down the street for him. The sun reflected off the street in waves. Somewhere a man was singing. Darius's disappearance worried me. I recalled how his life used to be full of intrigue with the neighborhood boys. The same ones he would be friends with and lavish high praise on would disappoint him by not including him in a game or by slighting him while he tried to fix a tire. Then he called them nasty names (son of a dog, or whoremonger) with the same intensity. Sometimes he got into ferocious fights with them. At thirty-one he had retained that adolescent quality, and would have it still at forty or fifty.

From the adjacent street a figure staggered into the light. I blinked, staring. It was Darius. He stumbled, blood trickling down his face, his hands pressed to his scalp.

I ran to him.

"What happened?"

He doubled over and then straightened up again. His face was dead white under the trickles of blood and his lower lip drooped and quivered.

I led him inside.

"Sons of bitches," he whispered, staring downward as we walked. "They've asked for it now."

"Who were they?"

"The two sons of bitches. I should have run them over last night."

"It was them? Oh, no!"

Darius sat by the pool and tried to wash his face with one hand. I noticed that his left hand and forearm were swollen.

"You're all bruised," I said.

"It's nothing," he said.

Water kept missing his face and blood continued gushing out.

"Let me do that for you," I said.

"It's nothing," he repeated.

"It seems bad to me."

I put one hand on the back of his head and filled the palm of my other hand with water. "Here," I said, "I can do a better job."

He hesitated and then gave in.

I splashed water into his face several times. Then I picked up a towel hanging on a rope along with some clothes and dried his face around the wounds. The blood kept trickling down.

"I think I'd better take you to a doctor," I said.

"I'll be all right," Darius said through pale lips.

"Look, the blood doesn't seem to stop."

"There's a doctor two blocks away. Just walk me over there."

"Let's go then."

He got up, held his head in his hands for a moment and then straightened up. I took his arm to lead him out.

"We'll be all right," I said.

Tony sat on the hard chair in my room, working on his paper with the deadline as Simin and I visited in the courtyard. Darius lay on the bed in his room, his back turned to us, listening to music. The injuries had been minor but the doctor said he should rest in bed for a day or two. He was restless, fidgeting. In another room, through a half-opened door, I could see my father lying on a mattress, his face slumped into misery, sulking even in his sleep. Ziba slept tentatively beside him as if ready to jump up at any moment.

"Oh, I'm glad we have a moment to ourselves, some peace and quiet," Simin said, looking down at a pillowcase she was embroidering.

"Yes," I said, not feeling the peace and quiet. Those rooms seemed to be gates to larger worlds, with each of the figures pulling at me, wanting something. And I still had not recovered from visiting with a horde of relatives that had dropped in one by one all morning and stayed through lunch. My uncle was conspicuously absent. I did not actually introduce them to Tony. They just looked him over and tried to say something welcoming and he nodded back at them politely. They asked me the usual questions about him —what he was doing sitting there working, why was he taking me back so soon, how come I had not taught him Persian. They gripped my arm, kissed me on the cheek, touched my hair. I thought of the time when I had met Tony's family and had been struck by the absence of touching.

Some of the relatives had brought children and the house was covered with debris and toys they had strewn around—watermelon seeds, cucumber peels, a mutilated rag doll half-hidden behind a bush, a plastic car without wheels. And all the noise the children had made running around the yard, in and out of rooms, falling and crying, losing a pacifier and shrieking, climbing on adults' laps.

Every time Tony looked out, the women would pull their *chadors* over their faces. After a while Tony stopped looking out. He had his lunch alone inside while my father and another male relative went into Darius's room and I stayed with the women outside. In a way that suited Tony since it gave him maximum time to work but I could not help feeling bad that he had been exiled by the women.

The lunch was lavish—different stews and rices, pickles, salads, various breads, and drinks—partly for Tony's sake since it was our last day.

"I've become so clumsy. I don't know what's the matter with me. I think I'm hurrying too much," Simin said, beginning to suck her right forefinger. She had pricked it with the needle.

"You're doing a good job." I looked with admiration at the colorful, circular designs she had made on the fabric. "I was never good with my hands."

"No, you used to spend your time reading. I see your husband is the same way." She leaned over and whispered, "He's very handsome, better-looking than in his picture. He's very different from us though, isn't he?"

"I don't know. That's hard to say."

"I shouldn't have said that, I guess."

She stared at the pillowcase. "Oh, no, I made a mistake." She pulled the thread out of the needle and began to undo some of the stitches. "I wish you had seen some of the things I bought with the money you gave to me. That was so kind of you." There was still no trace of embarrassment in her voice. "I bought a comforter, sheets, pillows, a whole set of bedding practically."

A smile came into her anxious face as her hands fluttered over the pillowcase. Her problems and pleasures suddenly seemed so real and substantial. There she sat, thin, pale, looking ten years older than her age, her breasts almost flat under her badly-cut dress, and yet so rooted in her way of life. Every day she woke to her children growing a bit, and tried to cope with their problems and little triumphs as well as her own. There were few moments of monotony in her days. She did not look at things from behind a glass screen, as I felt I did at times, but directly, receiving their full impact.

"Look, I bought a present for you." She reached in her pocketbook and took out a little green box.

I took the box and opened it. There was a leather pendant inside with a picture of a dancing woman painted on it.

"This is lovely," I said, putting it on. It was a perfect match for the green shirt I was wearing. "Thanks."

"It's just a memento," she said. Then abruptly she began to put her embroidery away in a bag and got up. "I think I'd better get going. It's late."

"How are you going back?"

"By bus."

"I'll walk you to it."

We went outside together. A cool breeze blew through the narrow street. A young man was rolling a tire ahead of him. A little girl walked very straight, balancing an oil lamp on her head.

On the wider street I could smell bread being cooked on hot gravel in a bakery. Simin and I embraced and kissed before she got on the bus.

I did not return to my father's house immediately. I stopped at spots I had frequented as a child—a little stationery store where I used to buy school supplies, a bakery with its display of sweets, the school with its heavy iron door. I put my head to the door and looked in. No one was in the yard. I had a recollection of myself standing there once alone, crying.

I had a little friend with whom I used to walk back and forth to school, accompanied by my father or Darius. Once, she and I had identical dresses made by a tailor—blue crepe-de-chine dresses with ruffles around the sleeves and collars —and we paraded the streets wearing them, self-conscious, as if the whole world was looking at us. We had a favorite game in which we were sisters. In the game, we always went on a long imaginary expedition somewhere far away, a place with vast rivers and vast mountains, shady forests and cool wide spaces. We rowed over a creek and found ourselves on that huge magical land. I heard later that she had gotten married, become very fat, and had four fat children. She could be passing me now among the crowd and I would not know her. I wondered where she was that day when I stood in the schoolyard, crying all alone—I was missing my mother.

I recalled trying to cross a busy street with my mother. Many cars, bicycles, horsecarts, went by, on and on. She held my hand and helped me across through a slight opening in the traffic. "You'll help me when I'm old and feeble, won't you?" she said. I shook my head vaguely, unable to comprehend the possibility that she would ever become old and feeble.

Other memories swarmed over me as I walked back through the crowded streets, where thin men brushed against me for a mere touch of a naked arm, where women clung to their *chadors* with resignation.

It was dusk when I returned. A mass of birds flew away above the courtyard. Kites dived in the air like fish. I went directly to my room.

"Did you get a lot done?" I asked Tony.

"A fair amount." He barely glanced at me.

I watched him, his mild but precise gestures, the controlled charm in his manner. This was the quality that seemed to draw women to him, that once had appealed to me so much. But now all that was dead for me. No, I could not put up the struggle needed to revive things between us. I could not go back with him, not now anyway, not until the spell of my own past had lifted.

I sat down on the floor and began to take out some of the things I had packed in my suitcase.

"What are you doing?" Tony asked. "We have to leave for the airport soon."

"I'm not going."

"I knew you'd start on that again. It's him, the doctor, as I suspected. Maybe you deserve someone like him. An Iranian man who'd order you around, who'd be out every evening with his buddies while he left you at home to keep house for him. It's slavery for women here, as you well know. They wouldn't even let you out without a letter of permission from me." He stood up and began to pace the room. "The least you could do is to be honest with me."

"Have we ever been honest with each other?"

"I thought so." His voice was flat. His face seemed drained of emotion. He put the paper in his suitcase. Then he shut the suitcase and picked it up. "I want to go to the airport now. Are you coming or not?"

I shook my head.

"Do you at least understand the insanity of this?" He added more gently, "You've been brain-washed somehow. You were ill and people took care of you. It's natural to get attached to one's doctor under such circumstances. You must have been very frightened and I wasn't around to help you."

"I keep telling you it isn't the doctor. It has to do with the changes in me. Can't you understand that?"

"What about me? Where do I figure in all this? Do you realize how selfish you're being?"

"I'm sorry."

"This trip was a mistake for you."

I did not say anything. I was not being evasive. I really had no answers.

He paused by the doorway. He was furious. "You'll come back when you realize your mistake." He turned and left.

I watched him on the street, aching with every inch of distance between us. He walked with the suitcase in one hand and the briefcase under his other arm. His shoulders were hunched, his walk no longer had its usual grace. Hunched, lost in a private pain. I had failed him. We had failed each other.

20

"Aren't you supposed to go to the airport?" My father looked around for Tony. "What happened to him?"

"He left."

"Are you staying? I thought you might." He sounded triumphant rather than surprised. He shouted to Ziba and Darius. "Feri is staying."

Ziba was in Darius's room. They came to the doorway, Darius still wearing bandages on his face and arm.

"Are you really staying?" Darius asked.

"Her husband has already left," my father replied for me.

"Feri, I knew you belonged to us," Darius said.

In a moment he and Ziba came into my room. We all stood around as if waiting for an important meeting to start.

"He was a cold man," Darius said.

Ziba bent and touched my nightgown lying on the floor. I had not put things away after I had pulled them out of my suitcase. "Look how pretty American things are," she said. She got up and added, unexpectedly, "Every day that I wake I say to myself, another long day and I'm still alive to endure it."

I wished I could tell her that I meant to leave for Kashan

almost immediately, knowing that much of her sadness came from my decision to stay. Instead I said, "You need a little vacation. You've been working so hard."

"Yes, I'll take you on a vacation," Darius said.

"Ah, you are a good son," Ziba said. "But you'd better go back to bed now and rest."

Darius looked very pale, but instead of going to his room he sat on the floor with his legs stretched out. He fumbled in his pocket for a cigarette. He found one, lit it, and began to smoke in a deliberately mannered way.

"It's your fault that he gets himself into trouble all the time," my father said to Ziba. "You spoiled him. He only wants to play and fight."

"What's wrong with him, he's better than all the boys in the neighborhood."

"Don't talk about me," Darius protested.

"Nobody is ever satisfied with anything I say or do," Ziba complained.

"Mother, be quiet," Darius said, flicking the cigarette ashes on the rug. "There's never an ashtray anywhere in this house."

"I have to get some work done," Ziba said, starting to leave. "Darius, are you sure you don't want to go back to bed?"

"I'm sure. I feel much better." He pressed the butt of his cigarette against the uncovered spot on the floor. Then he got up and looked at himself in the little mirror on the mantel, rubbing his hand gently on the bandage and then stroking his chin. "In a day or two I'll be able to get out and kill those whoremongers."

"Are you crazy?" my father said, sighing resolutely and sitting at the edge of the bed.

Darius turned away from the mirror and sat down, this time on the chair.

"I know what you ought to do," he said to me. "Teach school. They can use people like you here."

"That's exactly the kind of thing she's suited for," my father said. "You can help schools to do things better."

"I don't want to worry about that for a while."

"There's no hurry. Take your time and do what you think is best," my father said.

Ziba came into the courtyard and began to polish a brass pot. My father gazed at her for a moment and said to Darius, "You should come and work with me in the shop. Not like the last time though. You just sat and watched the girls."

Darius laughed.

"I'm going out to buy some sweets to celebrate Feri's stay."

"I'll go with you," Darius said.

I had a frightening dream that night. Tony was running through a tunnel and I followed, struggling to catch up with him. A bright light shone through the tunnel and a sound like thrashing of wind against trees roared through it. Tony's body seemed transparent in the light, shining with a garish blue color. It seemed urgent that I reach him. I did not quite know why. As I kept running the light became so bright that I could no longer see him. Finally I came to the end of the tunnel and found myself in a blind alley with a row of garbage cans along its sidewalks. Cats were walking together, slowly, harmoniously, like flocks of sheep. I saw someone who looked like Tony curled up in a corner. I ran over, but there was only a stiff suit with no body inside of it.

I woke, shivering.

Then I fell into a heavy sleep with no dreams and next time I woke it was dawn. Tony would be back in Lexington by now. I wondered what action he would take about getting us back together or if he would wait for me to do so. He might not take me back if I went to him. The thought gave me no real pain.

There were the obvious reasons for my wanting to stay on—dissatisfaction with Tony, my job, a yearning to spend more time with my mother and make up for what was already lost, a need to delve deeper and deeper into my past. But as I lay there in early dawn, I realized there was another reason. As the days went by I had begun to learn not to panic about unplanned time. How nice it would be to wake in the morning and know that time was my own, and be able to enjoy it.

A rooster crowed. A muezzin began to call people to prayer. I used to love waking at dawn to those sounds and watching my mother rising and bending in prayers. Her face, surrounded by her *chador*, seemed infinitely peaceful and benevolent. I would lie in bed, my eyes half-closed, and follow the rhythm of her movements. My father prayed earlier so that he could leave for the bazaar. I never saw him pray at that hour.

Later in the day I wrote a letter to my director, telling him I was taking an indefinite leave and therefore did not expect to be hired back if I returned. He was a tall, gray-haired man who always looked distracted behind his glasses. He had become famous while he was still a graduate student for synthesizing simple enzymes, and was now working on more complex hormones.

I tried to picture his reaction to my resignation. He

would be disconcerted and surprised at first and then would say women are risks.

After sealing the letter I began to pace the room. Ironically my head was suddenly full of ideas for experiments.

21

"You think I haven't suffered?" my father asked, going to the edge of the roof, sulking.

Before us stretched an expanse of other rooftops, mosquito nets, beddings, clothes hanging on ropes, ornate chimneys and parapets.

"I know you have. But I have to spend some time with my mother." I went over to him and looked down into a courtyard across the street. A young, paralyzed girl used to live there. Her mother and brother would lift her by her legs and shoulders every evening and carry her into a room to bring her out again the next morning. Sometimes she would wail and rapidly move her head. Her brother was a heroin addict, a gaunt, middle-aged man who sat for long hours by his sister's bed, his back stooped, his head lowered.

"Go then, if that's what you want," my father said, and began to cough, his face growing red. When the coughing subsided he said, "I have hopes of your marrying a nice Iranian man, having children. Of your becoming the head of a school. That would please all of us."

"I can't think that far." I would live on some of the money Tony and I had saved and let the future rest for a while. I heard footsteps. It was Darius holding a paper kite, shaped like a lantern.

"How nice it would be to fly away with just a touch of the wind," he said, letting the string go.

"What are you doing flying that kite," my father asked, looking up, squinting.

"I'm having a good time," Darius said, turning to me. "Come and hold this. The wind is just right."

I took the spool in both hands. The string pulled hard as the kite moved up rapidly, translucent in the sunlight.

My father watched us for a moment, shook his head and left.

Darius stared at me as I held the kite, watching it go higher and higher. I became aware of his arm touching mine, furtively. I moved away slightly. His arm touched me again.

"I think I'm going down," I said. "I'm getting tired of this."

"No." A single word, uttered in almost a whisper.

I looked up at him. His expression was the same as it had been years before when he had attacked me on the stairs leading up to that roof.

"Here," I said. "Take this."

He took the spool and my hand with it. I tried to pull my hand away, but he held on very hard.

"What are you doing?" I asked.

He did not answer. His eyes were fixed on my face.

Then, suddenly, he let go. "I'm sorry," he said, and walked away.

The kite was wavering and coming down. My hand shook as I held the spool more firmly. The kite began to go up again, up and up, until it became a tiny red spot. Behind it an orange streak spread over the horizon, fading by the minute.

22

It was midafternoon when I got to Kashan and the heat, the glaring sun, had driven most people off the streets. On the lane leading to my mother's house a man in faded clothes lay on the ground in a shady strip made by the wall. His lips were wide apart and flies played on them. The street was quiet and empty.

The door to my mother's house was open and I went in, but neither she nor my uncle was at home. I went to the room she had fixed for me before. It was as I had left it, wrinkles on the blankets, a pair of slippers by the bed, a clay bowl. The objects floated in sunlight.

I waited in the room. Then I saw my mother coming, limping a little, as if in pain. Her face had that blank, bloated look. I could not wait until I saw a smile reflected on it—her smiles were so sparse.

"Mother," I called to her.

She looked at me, a little puzzled, but soon she smiled with recognition which came quickly this time.

"You're back," she said, walking rapidly towards me. "What happened?"

I came out and sat on the steps by the doorway. "Nothing happened," I said. "I just wanted to stay with you for a while." So much had happened and yet nothing that I could easily put into words.

Two days later I ran into Mahmood Majid near a mosque. It had rained that morning and the heat had abated somewhat. The buildings sparkled. Children played noisily on the streets, relishing the change of the weather.

"Feri, Feri."

I turned around. Mahmood Majid stood in the midst of a crowd of people rushing out of the mosque and scattering in different directions. I waited until he caught up with me.

"What are you doing here? I came over one day and your mother said you had left."

"I decided to stay here, for a while."

He looked at men who stared at me as they passed by. "We'd better get away from here."

I followed him to a quieter street.

"Would you like to sit somewhere?"

"O.K."

We walked to a tea house a few blocks away.

We sat in the little courtyard in the back, where a fountain splashed into flowers and bushes. A feathery old hen hopped around in the water. From a room across the yard a woman came out and began to sweep the ground.

"This is a lovely place, isn't it?" Mahmood Majid said.

"It is." A pleasant lassitude had come over me.

Two children came out of the room and began to run up and down the stone steps in front of it, making a clop-clopping sound with their wooden slippers. The woman told them to go back in. They ran in, laughing hard, almost out of breath.

The waiter came over and greeted Mahmood Majid. We ordered tea.

"A family runs this place—different sons take turns working. He's the oldest son."

"I like restaurants like this—family and business combined."

"Some of the restaurants in the United States are like that." He thought for a moment. "It's odd how dreamlike the United States seems to me now—not as though I spent twelve years there."

"You've never gone back for visits?"

"No." He shook his head. "Every year I've thought of going but when the time comes I get involved with something else. I guess I don't particularly want to go back."

"You seem to have made a life for yourself here."

He took a few gulps of his tea and said, "You know, when I came to your mother's house and you weren't there I was really disappointed."

He was looking straight at me. I was weakened with desire. His eyes were so clear and unflinching—the eyes of a young boy almost, unperturbed.

In a flash, I saw my mother years ago going to meet the man she loved. She meets him on the shadowy corner of an alley, a dark stairway, or behind a hidden tree. He looks something like Mahmood Majid but more dapper, wearing a dark-blue suit with a red handkerchief in his breast pocket. They greet each other warmly. The air is moist and sweet-smelling. They stand and look at one another for a long, long time. Then he whispers, "You come with me and I promise to make you happy, happy forever." The sheer sound of his voice makes her tremble. There is fear and confusion in her eyes. For once she lets her *chador* slip down over her shoulders and they kiss, shivering in each others' arms.

When I looked back at Mahmood Majid he had lowered his eyes and was staring at something on the ground. Hundreds of tiny red ants crawled away. The one at the beginning of the line carried a bread crumb, almost the size of himself, in his mouth.

"Look how straight they crawl."

"Yes," I said, aware of a tiny ache at the wavering of his attention from me.

"It's very funny," he said, turning to me. "But I feel I can tell you anything, anything at all. That's what I liked about you immediately. You and I have a lot in common. We both have tried living in the West and have been disappointed." He laughed, perhaps thinking he sounded too serious. "Don't you think?"

I nodded.

Some men came in and sat not far from us. They greeted Mahmood Majid. Everyone seemed to know him. He belonged so much in these surroundings. I had seen Tony the same way, only in another context.

Mahmood Majid began to stir the thickened sugar at the bottom of his tea glass with a spoon. I watched him with the same ache I had felt a moment ago when he had looked at the ants.

He leaned very close to me. "That night when we were in the garden you seemed like a real Eastern woman. You looked and acted differently . . . it's hard to explain."

I waited for him to elaborate but instead he said, just as vaguely, "I don't want you to think I was being cold."

The awkwardness and the stiffness I had felt that night came back to me and I tried to fight it. I could see, behind my attraction to him, that a real conflict remained: he kept drifting in and out of a stage of my life that I had rejected and wanted to regain; he embodied the same pain, the same elusiveness.

"I think I know what you're saying," I said.

He searched my face. "I hope I didn't offend you. I see that I have."

"No," I said, willing myself to say no more. It would be self-defeating to begin to depend on him just as I wanted to pull so many strings together, think things through.

In a few moments I said, "It's getting late. I'd better go back."

He put a bill on the table and said, "Now that you're staying we'll see each other often."

I nodded hesitantly but said nothing.

Shops were now lit up and music blared out of radios. Horse-drawn carriages and donkeys trotted next to cars, making jingling sounds. We walked for a moment and then I raised my hand for a cab.

He waited until I got in. When I turned around after a block he was still standing there on the sidewalk.

23

My mother and I rode side by side on donkeys along with many other pilgrims travelling on foot, bicycle, and donkey. We were all going in the same direction, to the shrine of Zeinab, a poetess-saint. We had started out in the morning and now it was dusk. The sunset splashed against the sky. We were all quiet now as we were reaching the rest area before the shrine. My body ached from the long, bumpy ride. We passed the flat road, went up a hill and down again. From narrower paths, other pilgrims were joining us, making the main road very crowded and harder to travel on. The color of the sky faded quickly and stars began to come out.

Years ago I had gone on a pilgrimage with my mother. I sat in front of her on a donkey, with her hands around my waist. I would fall asleep and wake up to see the stars and the moon above and feel my mother's breasts like pillows.

Now I looked at her. From a whole day's hard travelling, the lines of her face were deepened. I reached out and touched her arm. "How do you feel?"

"A little tired," she said, her head shaking. "But we should be there soon."

On and off people would speak to each other and then fall into silence.

Lights began to glimmer before us and we reached a group of cafes, stalls, and shops lit by gas lamps. Behind them stood an immense field, surrounded by trees, with rivulets of water running through it. There were many tents of various sizes and shapes raised on the field, some no more than thin mosquito nettings or heavy cloth hung on trees. Men, women, and children were coming in and out of them.

We stopped there, giving our donkeys to one of the men who stood by a stall ready to take them and rent us a tent. Many of the other pilgrims stopped there as well.

One man led the donkeys to a pen. Another man took my mother and me to the tents, showing us the selection we could choose from. We took a small one, tied by ropes to four trees. Mattresses, pillows, blankets, and a jug of water and two glasses were the only things inside. A wide stream ran through the field in front of the tents, bright with the reflection of the moon, stars, and gas lamps. Some children came back and forth to get water in pots or jugs. In the center of the field several fires were built inside of stone stoves and people stood talking with each other and cooking. Groups of children sat around playing with marbles, rag dolls, or jumped over the chalked lines.

My mother lay down to rest while I went away to buy food for us. I zigzagged through the people and trees. Stones from the unpaved ground kept getting into my shoes and I had to stop from time to time to shake them out. No one noticed me. I was an Iranian woman, wearing a *chador*. Beyond the field there was a hill and many people had gathered on it. I went up the hill and joined the crowd. A group of musicians sat in the corner and began to play— violin, santur, and drums. A young woman with a rather sad face and coiling black hair began to sing, her voice rising to feverish heights at times. On the other side of the hill I could see the lights of some peasant huts showing behind trees.

I stood there for a while, listening, watching, my mind filled at the same time with other similar scenes from the past. I suddenly thought of my body as an immense shell, emptying from one side and filling from the other. The stars, the pink flowers on my *chador*, the knobs on the singer's black hair, the dark eyes of a young man standing in the crowd and smiling at me just then—were all little grains being fed into me. I took them in with each breath, slowly.

Then I walked to the shops and bought a leg of lamb, vegetables, fruit and yogurt, and wandered back. My mother was still asleep. I prepared the salad and then went to broil the meat on the fire. A couple of the women began chattering with me. They had come here for a vacation, visiting the shrine every day.

I came back with the meat and spread a sauce made with tumeric, onions, and yogurt over it. I arranged everything on plates we had brought with us and then woke my mother to eat.

"Do you think everything will be all right for you here in Iran? You've been with me for two months now," she said suddenly.

"I wasn't happy before. No matter what I do now it couldn't be any worse,"

"I hope so," she said. "I'm an old woman. I'll die soon. You have to think of yourself."

"I know," I said. "Everything seems simpler to me now."

FOREIGNER

At that moment I was so happy that I began to fear that something would happen to destroy it, something beyond my control.

After we ate I washed the dishes in the stream, then we went to bed. Soon it grew quiet, everyone climbed into tents and the gas lamps and fires were put out. The moon now reflected on the stony ground. The sound of the stream, the barking of dogs somewhere, and the jeering of insects took over. Listening to those sounds I fell asleep easily. I woke very early and felt the dew in the air and heard the stream again and the birds singing clearly in the trees. Children were waking up. A donkey brayed and rattled its chain.

I turned over and looked at my mother. Her face was serene in her sleep. I knew soon I would have to make decisions, think beyond the day, but for the moment I lay there. Tranquil.